DANNY SIGHED.
SANDY SCREAMED.

Suddenly the movie on the drive-in screen was less interesting than their new-found passion. Danny took Sandy in his arms and, in one clean sweep, had her struggling beneath him on the front seat of Greased Lightnin'.

"Danny, take it easy!" Sandy yelled. "I'm still the same girl I was last summer. Just because you give me your ring doesn't mean we're gonna go *all the way!*"

Sandy dove for the door.

"I'm sorry, Danny . . . maybe we better just forget about the whole thing."

Sandy took off the ring and threw it at Danny, then ran away in tears.

"Hey, Sandy," Danny yelled out the window. "Where you goin'? You can't just walk out of a drive-in!"

Books by Ron De Christoforo

Grease
The One and Only
A Small Circle of Friends

Published by POCKET BOOKS

By RON DE CHRISTOFORO

Based on the screenplay by
BRONTE WOODARD
Adaptation by ALLAN CARR
Based on the original musical by
JIM JACOBS and WARREN CASEY

POCKET BOOKS
New York   London   Toronto   Sydney   Tokyo   Singapore

POCKET BOOKS, a division of Simon & Schuster Inc.
1230 Avenue of the Americas, New York, NY 10020

Copyright © 1978 by Paramount Pictures Corporation

ISBN: 0-671-02456-6

This Pocket Books paperback printing April 1998

10   9   8   7   6   5   4   3   2   1

POCKET and colophon are registered trademarks of Simon & Schuster Inc.

Printed in the U.S.A.

In memory of Unk.

Special thanks to:

Carole B., Sally M., Monica S.,
and again to Kip Curren.

SUMMER'S
END

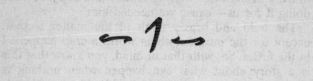

Now, TO TELL THE TRUTH, THE THING YOU GOT TO RE-
alize before you set out to read a story about the
fifties is that nothing ever happened. So, there is really
nothing to tell. Absolutely nothing of any importance.
Sure, some history books will say that some history
was made here and there in the 50's. Magazines'll
show you new appliances, a new war, fancy contrap-
tions, clothing, inspirational hobbies, and a lot of other
crap that kept people distracted. But this is a story
about people who didn't want to be distracted, at least
not by anything or anyone other than themselves. We
had each other and our music, and that was everything.

Yeah, the music—man, it kept us alive. It told our
stories, our dreams, and our heartaches. Our music
understood us. Elvis, Chuck, Jerry Lee, Buddy, The
Drifters, The Coasters, The Moonglows—they cared.
All you had to do was slip a coin into the slot and
you found somebody who knew what it was really
all about.

But the Big El, he really turned it around. Not
everybody understood him. I remember reading about
a car dealer in Cincinnati who advertised that he'd
break 50 Elvis records for every car he sold. In one

3

day, he sold five cars. But Elvis didn't care about some car dealer breaking his records, or the cops who stood in front of the stage waiting to take him away. He was doing it for us—'cause we needed him.

The bold and brassy truth of the matter is that, except for the music, nothing worth a crap happened in the fifties. So, with that in mind, you know that this is a story about what can happen when nothing is happening—a story about what kids do when there's nothing to do.

And Sonny-boy will tell you all about it.

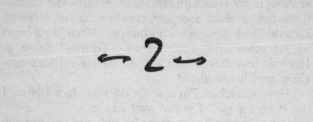

IT WAS THE LAST SATURDAY NIGHT OF SUMMER, BEFORE
school opened, and everybody was depressed. Deeply
depressed, I got to admit, even me, Sonny, who got
my name partly because I smile so much and partly
because I am the love of every loving lady, even me—
I got depressed. Ahh, Sonny-boy, I told myself, it's up
to you to keep the morale of these guys up. UP, UP,
UP!!! What would the Thunderbirds be without that
radiant smile of their good-times honcho, Smilin'
Sonny LaTierri? The boys need me to look up to, and
when they do I want to be smiling, ear to ear. I ain't
a hard guy, like Fierce Freddy, leader of the Flaming
Dukes, or Nasty Nicky from the Water Tower Gang.
The boys learned from me that a good personality and
a healthy attitude can go a long way longer than a
crapped-out face and a blackjack, any day.

Some of the boys were hanging on our corner,
bugged and disgusted. Kenickie was leaning against
the stop sign, smoking a Luckie, looking like he was
gonna fade away any minute, and happy in a sad way
about it. Even his tattoos seemed to lose their color.
The muscles he had worked so hard to build up were
drooping with his spirit.

Kenickie was wearing a sleeveless black T-shirt,

rolled-up dungarees, white socks, and black shoes. His arms were covered with tattoos of pictures and inscriptions like a black scorpion crawling up his forearm, Donald Duck smiling on his biceps, "Mom" in a heart on his other arm, and "Kenick—T-Birds" below it. His hair was slicked into a D.A., with a curlicue dangling over his forehead.

"Hey, Kenickie! Put a smile on your face before I put it on for ya!" I yelled over to him.

He hooked his hands under his belt and ignored me.

I could tell from the look on Kenickie's face that he needed a moment to be alone, a moment to figure his place in the world and to come face-to-face with the true meaning of summer's end, and I figured, as his friend, I had to give him that moment, and afterwards I had to keep him away from speeding cars. It was something all of us here tonight were feeling, like a stone weight upon our shoulders. The air was thick and sad, like a bad, late movie.

Tonight the boys were slipping fast into a funk and I didn't know what could pull them out of it. Even the Pink Ladies over at the Frosty Palace might not have helped tonight, although it was worth a try later on. But right now, even Kenickie looked soft.

Doody, named after Howdy because of his red hair, freckles, funny ears, and his lousy guitar playing, was slumped down on the steps staring off into space, looking hopeless. He was the youngest in our crowd and he was probably thinking that he had the most to lose once summer ended. Doody was usually a funnyman and a wise-cracker, but tonight he had the wind blown out of him.

Doody dressed a lot like a cartoon character. He mixed plaids and stripes, with red, orange, and green; he wore his baseball cap backwards, and two different sneakers. He tried to swirl his hair into a D.A., but it was so thick and curly it shot out into all different directions.

His mother's voice would be ringing through the air any minute now, as it was almost 9:30, and time for him to go home. He looked like he could almost hear her yelling, "DONNNNN—AALLD! Nine-thirrrrrty!" At which point, he'd groan and say, "I wish she'd stop calling me Donald in public. I tell her all the time," then push himself off the steps and head around the corner for home.

Roger really looked a mess. He was usually jumping in his boots about the next best way to beat the pinball machines at Augie's, but tonight he was straddling the fireplug, probably hoping for a fire to take his mind off things.

Roger was addicted to mooning. He'd do it anywhere for anyone. It sort of came over him like a spell. Before anyone knew what was happening, Roger would have his pants down and be shining his peachy moons right at you. He said he was working on trying to control himself, but he wasn't making much progress. I didn't even think that mooning somebody tonight would have helped him.

Usually, he was a pretty sharp dresser, but now his shirt was half undone, with the collar twisted, his pleated baggy pants were crumpled and he was sitting on the plug, with one foot on top of the other, combing his hair out of place. That was just about how we all felt—out of place.

Only Danny had enough sense not to come around tonight. Danny Zuko was the leader of the Thunderbirds. He had it all. The girls really went for the slick black hair, curled and pomped in the front, skirted back above his long sideburns, and flipped down in a tight D.A. in the back of his head.

Danny dug wearing just a white T-shirt with his leather, black pants, and boots. He was a pretty cool dude that a lot of chicks liked. But Danny was never interested in the chicks who chased him. Sure, he dug all the attention—made him feel like a big man, but that wasn't where his heart was at, though he never really showed it. He'd soak up all the sweetness the girls'd lay on him, then usually come back to the corner and hang out with the guys. He told a lot of stories about who was puttin' out what, but we knew, deep down, he was just telling stories. It was more to pass the time than anything else. We knew almost nobody was puttin' out, unless it was for their steady, but then you never heard anybody talk about their steady puttin' out.

Danny was the one who had the idea that we should call ourselves "The Thunderbirds" so everybody would know who we were. That was what made him our leader. We outfitted ourselves with leathers covered with zippers and buckles, and became the T-Birds.

As I think now about how Danny became the leader of the Thunderbirds, I realize he never competed for the spot. Never even spoke about it. It just sort of happened. And it wasn't so much that he led, but everyone else followed. He always had the look of someone with a place to go, a destiny already in hand, and aces packed up his sleeve. I don't think he even liked being the leader, and sometimes he would say as much, or just not show up around the corner because he would get bugged always having other guys and chicks waiting for him. But somewhere inside him, he enjoyed spearheading the troops.

So there we were, just hanging out, each of us going over the spent summer, wondering what happened, how it went, and whether or not it was really such a bad thing that school was starting next week.

So, Danny was home tonight. He'd been staying home a lot lately, pining away a summer love, and helping his old man at his store. But we all knew as soon as school started, Danny would be right back in the swing of things.

Then there was me, Sonny LaTierri. Like I said, some of the chicks thought I was a real hunk, with my black hat and black shades, black shirt and pants. The Midnight Rider was what they called me. Good-looking, dark and sexy, but not too tall. Yeah, they loved it. Dressing in black was kind of my trademark, and besides, my mother said it was easier on her washing my clothes. She wasn't crazy about my hair, shades, hat, and leather, but then, none of our mothers were too famous on our hair or clothes. My mother said it made a nice boy like me look like a hoodlum. I told her that was just the point. My old man never really said much about it. He was more interested in what I *did*. He was always asking questions. "Where ya been?" he'd ask. I'd answer, "Out." "I know that," he'd say, "but where?" "On the corner," I'd tell him. "Well, whadah ya do on the corner—every night, all summer long?" "Ehey, pop, whaddah ya think? What's there to do? Same thing you used to do on the corner—just hang out." "Oh," he'd say, and go back to watching "Gunsmoke."

I guess I should explain some things about the neighborhood and the corner, which was where we actually spent most of our time during the summer. The neighborhood was mostly corner stores, pool halls, arcades, and a lot of little houses on a lot of little streets. But street corners made up our lives. We marked our boundaries in street corners. Corners were where kids hung out and carried on the business and pleasure of their lives, which was mostly concerned with, you know, hanging out.

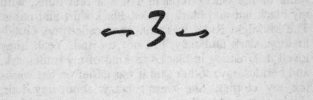

BEFORE I COULD GET TOO MUCH INTO MY THOUGHTS along came Betty Rizzo, the leader of the Pink Ladies. The Pink Ladies were our cronies in craziness. They hung out at the Palace, where we would go for a bite to eat or to see the Ladies.

The Palace was, well, like a neon nightmare that we had gotten used to. It was crudely shaped like an igloo, with a giant hamburger and bun, say about the size of a walrus, hanging over the arched doorway. Everything in the Palace was either white or pink, and had something to do with the polar region. The booths were shaped like chunks of ice and the juke box was sprayed to reflect the Northern Lights. The waitresses wore short fur-trimmed skirts with hoods, trying to look like Eskimos. The counters were floating chunks of pink ice. The floor was a pink sea. It was all kind of nauseating at first, and not a good place to even think of eating food, until you got used to it.

The whole place was Ernie's idea of heaven. (Ernie was the owner, bouncer, and cook—though he liked to call himself the chef.) To top off the effect, pink and white fluffy clouds (wads of cotton sprayed with paint and collecting grease and dust) hung in the main dining room. Actually, there was no main dining room.

That was what Ernie called the entire Frosty Palace—
the main dining room, as if there were more to the
place.

So, the whole Palace was icy white and pink, and
usually hot in the summer and cold in the winter. And,
also, there was nothing royal about the Palace, but
because it was mostly white and pink, Rizzo and her
girlfriends named themselves "The Pink Ladies," following suit to the Palace, and they took to dressing
mostly in pink.

Rizzo was a girl who, in her own hard-edged way,
was a real good looker. She was dark and fleshy, tough
and loud and wise-assed, but could, when moved, be
sweet with understanding.

She had big brown cow-eyes that could melt you in
a second, or narrow with meanness and freeze you
like a cube. Mostly she was a pretty good kid who
cracked gum all the time and spoke in spurts out of
the side of her mouth, between two luscious red lips.
She had fluffy teased black hair, thin penciled eye-
brows, and a face dusted with pancake and rouge. Tonight she wore a tight pink sweater, a black waist
cincher, and a long pink skirt—all of which brought
out the best in her beautiful body. She had her black
satin jacket thrown over her shoulder, which had
"THE PINK LADIES" embroidered in pink on the
back. All in all, she looked like a ripe wildflower.

She strolled up to the corner and said she was on
her way to the Palace to join the Ladies. As soon as
she was close enough to see us in the light from the
streetlamp, she knew we were in no mood to be irked.

Instead of mouthing off in her usual fashion, like,
"Ehey, ya fruity fags, 'smatter, yer zipper got yer
tongue?" she eased up to each of us in turn, put her
long lovely arms around us, and buried her head into
our necks and laid a deep, red, juicy hickie on each
of our necks. This done, amidst groans, gasps, and

11

grabbing at Rizzo's behind, she walked off, headed coolly toward the Palace, with not a hair out of place. Nice girl, Rizzo.

We were settling down from all the excitement Rizzo had caused just as Bobby Barrels zoomed up to the corner. It's not quite right for me to say he zoomed up, since you might think he was on wheels, which wasn't true. He was in his kicks beating the cement of the sidewalk, but when Barrels went anywhere, he zoomed. You could almost see his pistons pumping, his rods ringing, and his joints jostling while the exhaust steamed out of his mouth like a smokestack. He even screeched when he came to a stop.

Barrels was possessed by automobiles and women, and talked freely and without encouragement on both subjects. "She" could be the woman or the car, with greased linings, cushy springs, and a flooded carburetor. He revved her up, slipped the clutch, dropped her into reverse, and, the very next second, flatshifted from low to high gear like friggin' greased lightning, reeled around a crooked corner, giving her the juice, and rode her high and hard down Demon's Run, slamming on the brakes before he dropped his trans.

When Bobby was around, he was given about two minutes of sympathetic listening on the outside chance that he might have something of interest to say. But shortly after we'd realize that that couldn't be the case, he was cut off in mid-sentence as he was torquing up, with something like, "Hey, Bullshitface, enough!"

The real problem was that Bobby didn't have a car, otherwise he would have been a lot easier to take, and would certainly have been worth tolerating. But he did nothing to hide the fact that he had neither car nor driver's license, and his romantic adventures were also coming under grave suspicion. But somewhere he had accumulated a seemingly endless store of automotive facts and trivia which none of us were prepared or motivated to challenge.

Barrels' two minutes were just about up now, and Kenickie, simply and dryly and without addressing Barrels directly, said, "Cut the shit, Bullshitface!" to which Bobby Barrels laid rubber and sped away in another direction. He was, all in all, the biggest goddamn bore you'd ever want to meet.

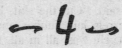

WELL, BEFORE I WAS PLEASANTLY (BY RIZZO) AND
rudely (by Barrels) interrupted, I was about to tell
you about how we spent the summer. Mostly it was
passed with games. Love games, street games, ball
games, card games, pool games, pinball, bowling, and
various inspired inventions. We played blockball,
stickball, sidewalkball, handball, wallball, curbball,
awningball, and then, after we exhausted most of the
conventional uses for a round rubber airball, we'd cut
it in half and play halfball. Other games included hide-
the-belt, Chinese torture, buck-buck, electrocution (a
high-wire challenge), and hand grenade (a war game
played with fresh eggs).

I even managed to sneak in a little vacation at the
beach. My Aunt Millie owned a rooming house at the
seashore, and at least once during the summer, on my
father's vacation, my mother, me, and my father would
visit her for a few weeks. It was one of those things I
had to do—you know how it is. We'd all go to the
beach together during the day, and all walk the boardwalk together at night. I felt like I was a hundred and
two and couldn't wait to get home. But every year for
as long as I could remember, that was what we did

for my father's vacation, and I didn't see anything that would change it, until this past summer.

I walked in the house about 10:30 after a night with the guys on the corner, and my father was sitting in his chair watching "Maverick" or "Cheyenne" or "Wyatt Earp" or "Broken Arrow" or one of the five hundred westerns that was on television then, and he patted the arm of his chair, meaning for me to sit next to him. As much as he got to me, he was really a good guy, and I had a feeling he had some good news for me.

"You wanna go down the shore?"

Oh no, I thought. I should have seen this coming. But what I didn't understand was why he was *asking*. He never asked me, he simply told me we were going, and when.

"With you and Mom, right?"

"Well," he said, "Aunt Millie just called me and asked if you could go to her place for a few weeks and help her out."

I started to say, "Ahh, Pop, what am I gonna do by myself . . ."

When he said to me, "I just talked to Danny's father, and he says it's okay if Danny comes with you." He smiled at me.

"You're kidding, right?" I knew he wasn't.

"No lie, son-a-mine."

Then he did something he hadn't done in years. He slapped me on the ass.

"Gonna be an all-expense-paid vacation, compliments of your old man!"

All I could say was, "Hey, Pop! You're all right!"

The old man had a way of surprising me like that, out of the clear blue. He was something.

The phone was ringing. It was Danny.

"Sonny, you believe it!"

"No, you?"

15

"No. What are they up to?"

"Beats me."

"Whaddah you think they want?"

"I can't figure it."

"Me neither."

"Hey, Danny, I think it's okay. I mean, from here it looks like no strings. Maybe your old man and mine decided it was time we cut loose for a little."

"What's your aunt like?"

"All aces."

"Really?"

"Yeah. Great cook. Neat lady. You'll like her."

"This is too much!"

"I know."

"Well, whaddah we got to do for your aunt?"

"Ahh, it's no big deal. Same thing I do when I go to visit with my parents. Help her change the beds, put clean towels and soap in the rooms. A little sweeping and cleaning here and there. Watch the desk for a few hours. All light stuff. Give us plenty of time on the beach and the boardwalk. It'll be a gas!"

"Well, how come we ain't there yet?"

Two days later we were on our way. My father was going to drive us to the bus terminal, after we said our good-byes to the guys on the corner. Me and Danny walked around the block and found Kenickie, Doody, and Roger hanging out. They weren't too happy about us getting away.

"What if something comes up?" Kenick asked.

"Like what?" I wanted to know. Nothing had come up all summer.

"Who knows? That's just the point." Roger was worrying now. "I mean, we don't expect nothing now, but what if? Huh? What if? Being ready for the unexpected is just what we got to be ready for!"

There was doom, death, and destruction in Roger's voice. The other guys were nodding in dreaded agreement behind him. They looked like they were already in mourning.

"And who knows?" Doody chimed in. "Who knows? Something might happen down there. And then what? How'll we know where to find you guys? And what if we're too late? Huh? Tell me, huh?"

"Dood, we'll send you a postcard, okay? We're staying at Sonny's aunt's. If you guys get lonesome for us, drop us a line. Better yet, send a telegram."

"Ehey," I said. "Listen, we're gonna cover the place like a blanket, and if we're lucky, we'll get to do some playing under the covers."

"Ahh, you guys," Doody said sadly, "I'm gonna miss you."

My old man left us at the bus station, after slipping me and Danny some pocket money, and giving Danny a handshake and me a hug. Danny looked a little weird at me after my old man left.

"Aww, he's okay, Danny. It's just something he never got over, and I don't know how to tell him I'm too old now to be hugged by my old man."

Danny shrugged his shoulders and turned up the collar of his leather, playing the rebel looking for a cause.

Danny was a hard guy to figure. You had to know him well in order to read him, and there was more than one volume to him. He never told you much about how he was feeling, or what was going on inside that head of his. But just to look at him, you knew he was always ticking. Sometimes it takes years to get to know someone well, and it can be nice taking things slow. My mother once showed me a picture of Danny and me standing naked in a playpen with our arms around each other. That's how far back we go. In fact, one day the guys on the corner were arguing about who knew who the longest, and I said short of being born together, Danny and I did. Well, everybody jumped on my case until I brought around the picture, which iced everybody, including Danny. He looked at the picture, laughed, and said, "I guess it's too late now to break a set, huh?" And that said it all.

Here we were on the bus together for our summer fling. We passed the time with a kid in the back of the bus with a guitar who was doing some numbers. He was doing a lot of hot stuff on that ax of his and we just joined in. We did some harmonies on "Let the Good Times Roll" by Shirley and Lee, "In the Still of the Night" by the Five Satins, "Turn Me Loose," by Fabian, and a batch of Little Richard starting with "Tutti Frutti" and ending with "Long Tall Sally." We were really going great, all the way down to the shore.

When we got off the bus, we had lunch at the White Castle and tried to plan a strategy. It was raining.

"Ehey, Danny, where you think the best place for action is?"

"You mean girls?"

"What else?"

"Yeah, well, probably the beach."

"It's raining."

"I can see that. I guess we'll just have to wait on the sun."

"How long?" I was getting nervous.

"Whaddah I look like, a weatherman? How should I know how long?"

"I'm just trying to work myself up for this, you know! Can't go into this thing cold. Got to have some good lines in hand. We should work on it while the weather's lousy. Danny, you play the girl."

"Ehey, Sonny, relax. That's all you got to do, relax. When the spirit moves you, the words'll come, don't worry. And I ain't playing no girl."

"Think we should split up?"

"Huh?" Danny was confused.

"I said, do you think we should split up?"

"What the hell for?"

"I don't know, maybe play the percentages. What's our chance of finding two girls together?"

"In the rain?"

"Naw. On the beach, later."

"Same as finding one, or none." Danny had a point.

"A'right. The word is—*relax.*"

"You got it. When it happens, it'll happen, and we'll be right there not to miss a trick. Get it?"

"Got it."

"Good."

The White Castle waitress, a young college girl, brought us our sandwiches. I started shifting around in my seat. I thought she might be the one. I looked over at Danny. He shook his head.

By the time we got to Aunt Millie's, the rain had stopped, the sky had cleared, and the sun was pouring down. Aunt Millie was waiting in the kitchen for us. She gave us kisses and hugs and poured us each a beer. Like I said, Aunt Millie was all aces.

There were five floors in the rooming house, with about four rooms on each floor. If we got an early start, we could knock off and hit the beach by noon. The first day's work was a breeze—a little sweeping and straightening up, some routine jobs, and we were sprung.

Aunt Millie gave us a room on the top floor. It was her way of saying she didn't think she had to keep too close an eye on us, which could have been a mistake. Anyway, Danny and I were getting ready for the beach, and I was having a hard time convincing Danny that he really couldn't wear his leather to the beach.

"Why not?" he wanted to know.

I thought for a minute and realized that he could care less about sweltering in it.

"Who's gonna watch it when we go in the water?"

"I'll only go in to my waist."

So, there was no getting him out of his jacket. He went barechested beneath his leather and wore a pair of black swim trunks.

I had on a black T-shirt and black trunks. We both went in shades and barefoot, carried our towels around our necks and had our combs sticking out of our waistbands. We were ready to head for the beach. Outside, the pavement burned our feet, and when we got to the beach the sand was even hotter. We had to stop every few feet and stand on our towels. Finally we parked our stuff in the middle of a crowd of people. We were surrounded by blankets, umbrellas, kids, buckets, sand castles, water holes, and *girls*. God! So many girls!

"Danny, you see! Cheez, I can't believe it! Which one you like? I'll take the redhead, you can have her girlfriend, okay? Wait! What about the one in the striped bathing suit?" I knew I was going a little bit crazy, but I couldn't help myself.

"Ehey, Danny-boy, I think that chick in the white is giving you the eye."

In all this craziness and heat, Danny was cool as the iceman.

"Sonny, what's the word?"

"Yeah, relax, but look-it!"

Danny flipped up the collar of his leather and looked out into the ocean, like he was stranded alone on the beach waiting for his ship to come in, and not in any particular hurry about it.

In less than a minute, the girl in the white bathing suit was standing next to Danny.

"Yeah, real nice day," Danny said, without even looking at her. He continued to stare at the waves.

I walked over to Danny and the girl.

"Listen, the reason my friend here seems a little distant is that he's, well . . . relaxing." I smiled at the girl. She had a nice face. Blue eyes. Blonde hair. Great body. She smiled back, then walked away.

"See, man, you with all that crap about 'relax, relax,' we blew it! We didn't even have to move off the blanket, and we still managed to blow it!"

"Ehey, Sonny—"

"Yeah, I know, relax. You're so friggin' relaxed you're gonna fall asleep standing up. And if you want to know the truth, you look like an idiot standing there like a sun god in a leather jacket and bathing suit."

Danny shot me a look, then tore after me. I ran for the water. Danny stopped in his tracks, looking from the ocean back to our towels, then he peeled off his leather, wrapped our towels around it, and dove into the water.

We had a good time at the beach, even though we were shut out. We spent most of the day lying around on our towels. I yelled to a couple of girls who were sunbathing nearby, but they ignored me. Danny fell asleep smiling.

That night we had to work the front desk for my aunt from seven to eleven. There wasn't much to do except sit there and shoot the breeze, read comics, and say hello and good-bye to people as they came and went. Nobody checked in or out. It was a terrible night. After the nightman relieved us, we sat on the porch watching the people heading home from a night on the boardwalk, carrying stuffed animals, gee-gaws, cotton candy, and their sleepy little kids.

A middle-aged couple walked by with their daughter, who was about our age, blonde, pretty, and pure. Danny shot up to his feet and jumped on the railing. The blonde girl caught him out of the corner of her eye. Danny smiled shyly and gave her a tiny wave of his hand. It was corny as hell. The girl smiled back, then followed her parents into their hotel, next door to us.

"Damn, Sonny! She's the one. I know it. Something went 'pop!' "

Danny was pacing around the porch, babbling like an idiot.

"I got to do something. I gotta figure a way. I gotta—"

"Relax," I said, cutting him off.

Danny stiffened when he heard my voice, then he eased back his shoulders, threw out his chin, and strolled over to his chair again.

"Ehey, you got it, Sonny-boy, *relax.*"

He plopped in the chair and had to force his eyes away from the hotel which the blonde girl had entered.

Before going to bed that night, Danny stood a long time at the window of our room looking out at the hotel where the girl slept.

The next morning I had to run some errands for ol' Aunt Mil downtown, which left Danny to make the rounds in the house himself. I got back early in the afternoon and found Danny sitting on the porch, drinking a soda and talking to Blondie. Man, she was really cute. She had this soft silky hair, and white creamy skin, big blue eyes, and a great body. Her legs were a little red from the sun, but they looked great anyway. She had on a white terrycloth beach dress and white sandals.

Danny didn't see me coming up, so I caught something he was saying about him going to a private school in the suburbs.

He stopped short when I leaned over the railing and gave out my best smile.

"Ahh, Sandy, I'd like you to meet my best friend, Sonny."

"Hiya, Sonny!" Sandy said. "Danny told me lots about you."

"Lies, lies, lies!" I said. She laughed. Danny was

shaking his head, smiling, 'cause he knew that his girls always liked me best. But there was something special about this one. She had sparkle, and had touched off something in Danny. He was dazed. But Sandy was so far from any of the other girls Danny had dated, I really didn't know why all of a sudden Danny had flipped on her.

I figured they needed to be alone, so I went in and told Aunt Mil about what was happening with Danny and Sandy. I knew she would be able to work something out, and she did. She invited Sandy to come out with me, Danny, and her that night, to eat something and hear some music. Sandy was really excited and ran next door to tell her parents. Aunt Mil charmed the pants off Sandy's father, invited him and her mother in for a beer, and everything was set for that night. Everything except me having a date, but Aunt Mil told me that there were plenty of nice young girls at Cy's and that I was sure to meet someone—and Aunt Mil didn't lie.

Sandy showed up in this fluffy ruffled dress, looking more like she was going to the prom. Me and Danny both hung up our leathers for the night and sported windbreakers and, what else, T-shirts, jeans and boots. Aunt Mil was spiffed up, and made me feel kind of neat being on the arm of an older woman.

Cy's was a loud, flashy joint with records hung on the walls and ceiling and a juke that was playing Chuck Berry when we walked in. Aunt Mil was right about the girls at Cy's—there were so many they were dancing with each other. And one look at the guys told me there wasn't going to be much competition for me to beat out.

This big old fat guy with a bald head came running over to us in his varsity sweater and sneaks and gave Aunt Mil a hug and a kiss. It was Cy. He was an old friend of Aunt Mil's—a childhood sweetheart, she said. Cy gave us Cokes on the house and showed us to a booth near the juke. As we were sitting, Aunt Mil told us that her and Cy were going next door for a drink and would be back later.

I took my Coke and left Danny and Sandy alone together in the booth and walked to the counter, giving the place the once-over. In the corner booth there was a cute little number sitting alone flicking the ashes from her cigarette into the rolled-up cuff of her jeans. Now there was a woman I could love. I dipped slightly as I sauntered to the juke, and gave her a deep meaningful look as I passed by. After I played a couple of tunes, I turned and curled my head in her direction.

"Anything in particular you wanna hear . . . babe?"

Damn! I was so cool I could hardly stand it. I was the iceman waiting for the big thaw. Melt me! Please!

She walked over to the juke, gave half a smile, and instead of picking out a number, she took my hand just as "Why Do Fools Fall In Love?" came on the box. We danced. God, it was like a movie. I was in love!—The fool I was.

Her name was Marsha and she had started out the night with her brother, who deserted her, which she thought was the best thing that had happened all night—until me.

I have to admit I was a little stiff and nervous, since it had been a while since the last time I danced, but Marsha was getting me loose. Dancing with a girl was a great way to get to know her.

"Hey, Marsh," I said to her softly. "You dance like a dream."

I couldn't believe I said something as stupid as that, but there it was, and too late to take back.

She giggled and said, "Sonny, with you it's like walking on air."

I held her closer. Danny once told me that in spite

of myself, somehow I have a way with women. He's right.

After the song, we both went to the juke, holding hands, and played just about everything on it. We picked some slow numbers, like "Girl of My Dreams" by The Crests and "I Only Have Eyes for You" by The Flamingos, and we hit a lot of hot numbers like "Tweedle Dee" by LaVern Baker, "Roll Over Beethoven" by Chuck Berry, and a pack by the Big El.

I took Marsha over to meet Danny and Sandy, who were both watching us. I introduced everybody all the way around and said, "C'mon, let's cut a rug!"

We hit the dance floor just as "Blue Suede Shoes" came up. Sandy had a hard time of it at first, but she managed to pick up the back beat and start rolling. We shimmied, short-stepped, flipped and turned, changed partners once and then back again. We brought everybody in Cy's to their feet and dancing. The booths emptied and the dance floor filled. Skirts were swayin', bodies rockin'—the whole place was shakin' and nothin' could stop it.

Cy and Aunt Mil came in doing the jitterbug and everybody circled around them, dancing and clapping. Danny cut in on Cy and took over the floor with Aunt Mil. It was amazing. Danny held her by the waist and swung her from side to side around his body. Marsha took Cy by the hand and coaxed him back into the circle. Sandy and me started a line dance going up and down both sides of the dance floor, with Danny and Marsha and Cy and Aunt Mil in the middle. We couldn't sit down.

We must have danced through every number on the juke at least twice before we left Cy's that night. Marsha decided that her brother wasn't coming back, so we walked her to her hotel. She said she was leaving Atlantic City the next day, so I got her phone number and told her I would call, and we would go out. It turned out that she had just moved in a few blocks from me back home. That's the way these things go— you gotta travel to meet somebody who lives around the corner from you. I gave her a quick peck on the cheek and held her hand for a second before leaving.

So Aunt Mil was back on my arm and Danny and Sandy were walking behind us as we headed back to the house. We said goodnight outside, then Aunt Mil went in, and Danny walked Sandy next door to her hotel. I waited for him on the porch. They were standing an awful long time together just looking at each other, barely touching hands. I couldn't hear what they were saying, but I didn't have to.

One look at Danny when he came over to the porch told me that he was fogged in. He jumped up to the railing and straddled it.

"Sonny, I can't believe it! If I didn't know better, I'd say I was in love with her. Hell, I *don't* know better, and I am in love with her."

"Danny, know what? Me too."

"WHAT?"

"With Marsha. I'm in love with Marsha."

"Feels good, don't it?"

"I'm not sure."

"Whaddah you mean?"

"Well, we just met two really nice girls, and we both like them a lot, and we think they both like us a lot, right?"

"Yeah . . ."

"And we just had a terrific night, dancing and messing around and talking, right?"

"Yeah . . ."

"And the two girls even like each other a lot, and to top it all off, ol' Aunt Mil had the time of her life."

"Yeah . . ."

"Well the point is, if everything was so perfect, how

come it's down to you and me sitting here alone together again?"

"Ahh, it don't matter anyway." Danny had suddenly lost all of his kick.

" 'Smatter, Danny-boy?"

"She's out of my league, Sonny. Out of my territory. It was good for one night, but we're worlds apart. Besides, she's leaving in another day. I guess this fling is flung."

"Ahh, Danny, that don't sound like you."

"Sonny, she's a nice girl. What's she want with me?"

"Danny . . . you're a nice guy."

We both had a hard time sleeping that night. I was worrying about when I would see Marsha again, and Danny was worrying if he would see Sandy again, after school started.

The next day was Sandy's last, so Aunt Mil gave Danny the day off. Danny went to see her for what he said was the last time. A few hours later he returned like he had been through a suicide mission, tattered and in pieces.

I was sweeping the porch when he walked up.

"Well?"

"Well, what?" Danny tried to smile.

"Didja get her number?"

"Nawh. Too far, man. Like I said, out of my league."

"Danny, so what if she lives a hundred miles away? We could make weekend jags up there once in a while."

"Naw, Sonny, it's that, but it's not. The miles ain't the thing, it's the distance." Danny could be puzzling without wanting to be. "Yeah, the distance." Danny got this faraway look in his eyes.

We spent the rest of the week working around the house and sunning on the beach. Neither of us was really up for chasing any more girls, at least not until we were back on our own turf.

Aunt Mil knew that, more than anything, we wanted to get back to the guys and the neighborhood, so we finished off the week working and left with bags full of fudge and saltwater taffy, on a bus bound for the corner.

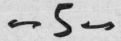

THE GUYS WERE FLIPPED OUT WHEN WE RETURNED. They asked a lot of dumb questions, like how many times did we get action. But it was really good to be home and with the guys.

I called Marsha the first day back and told her to come around and meet the rest of the guys. They made her feel like one of their own, which to a lot of girls would have been frightening, but Marsha felt loved.

We took her over to the Frosty Palace and introduced her to Rizzo and the other Pink Ladies, and in no time at all they were hitting it off like long-time pals. Rizzo told Marsha to come around whenever she wanted, and took her phone number just to make sure.

We were all one big happy crowd, except for Danny. He never quite seemed to pull himself out of this thing he had with Sandy. I never said anything to the other guys, but I knew he was losing his confidence. When the girls at the Palace came on to him, he'd turn off. When the guys on the corner tried to boost him up, he'd fold like he was holding a kangaroo straight in a poker game. It was at about this time that the T-Birds started to turn to me for reassurance. They began to get shaky. There was talk and rumors.

"Corner's gone to pot," Kenickie said, sitting down on the hood of a parked car. "Pretty soon there ain't gonna be nothing left but the stop sign."

"Yeah," Roger added, "I see it just like Rome went. Our Leader takes a powder, and so go his men. What a tragedy."

"I saw it coming. I tell you, I saw it coming." Doody was pacing around the stop sign trying to convince himself of his prophetic powers.

Me, well, in the clutch I'm at my best. You won't believe this, but you know what turned the tide? Kid stuff. We had outings, picnics, softball games, trips to the zoo, boat rides and parties, and as dumb as it sounds, it worked. We did everything together, which brought Danny out of his heartbreak. The Ladies would do the food, and the T-Birds would bring the sixes-of-suds along.

It was getting near the end of August when a well-meaning plot was laid by me and Marsha. I was over at the Palace with Marsha when I noticed a letter sticking out of her *Teen* magazine. It was an old letter from Sandy. What a break! Marsha and Sandy had been writing to each other all summer.

"And all this time, you never said nothing? Yooh, Marsh, what'samatter with you? I don't believe it!"

And I couldn't.

"Ehey, don't get pissy with me. What was there to say? I write to Sandy, she writes back. Big deal. What's it to you anyway?"

Marsha was missing the point of all this.

"But, what about Danny?"

"Oh, she asks about him, but she doesn't want me to tell him that she writes. She says if he was interested in her he'd have gotten her address himself."

"Interested?! You get *interested* in butterflies, stamps, and weird new diseases. Interested in her?? Damn! He's not interested in her, he's in love with her!"

Marsha began to see my point.

"I didn't know, Sonny. What can I do?"

"Write to her. Tell her we're coming up this—naw, make it next weekend. Me, you, and Danny. I'll get my cousin's car, for about ten years' worth of favors, but I'll get it and we'll make the trip."

"Boy, Sonny, wait'll Danny hears!"

"NO!!!" I didn't mean to scream. Everybody in the Palace turned. I smiled and waved to them.

"No, Marsh, we can't tell him. He'd never go. Not now. He's too proud for his own good. We'll say we're going to visit your old neighborhood, and . . . what?"

"And, I want him to meet my best girlfriend!"

"Great! Now get that letter off! Shit, sometimes I think I should have been a genius."

The following Saturday we packed Cousin Finn's '56 Chevy with sandwiches and six-packs of suds and headed up the turnpike. We had the radio blasting WAXX, and Vinnie Fontaine's program, "Pounds of Sounds" was on. He was hitting us with more than we could take: The Platters, Little Anthony, The Drifters, Sam Cooke, and plenty of the Big El. Vinnie himself was a gas.

"Hey, all you yon teenagers, if you're having fun, you're number one! If you're down, I'll get you on the rebound! If you're alone, call me on the phone! So keep your bean clean, and your feet neat, 'cause when I'm jockin' there ain't no stoppin'."

Vinnie played "Rock and Roll Is Here to Stay" and we drank and sang along with the top-down convertible sound coming up all around.

Marsha sat between me and Danny in the front seat,

and from time to time she would nudge me and smile over our little conspiracy. It was a beautiful summer day with the sun bearing down on us, the green countryside sparkling, and the wind in our faces. It was just about the most of the most. Danny had the first smile I had seen in a long while on his face.

We were cruising at fifty, feeling cut-loose and free, and whomping out on the suds and the music. Danny and Marsha were doing a harmony on "Earth Angel" just as I turned onto the exit. While we were waiting for a light at an intersection, I asked Marsha for directions. She dug into her purse and took out an old letter from Sandy.

"Stop at that gas station and ask directions," she said.

" 'Smatter, you forgot where you used to live?" Danny asked suspiciously.

Marsha, I learned, was not great on the ad-lib. She stammered and then turned to me in desperation. I pulled into the station, shut the motor, walked around to Danny's side of the car, leaned over and put my arm around his shoulders.

"Danny-boy, me and Marsha wanted to surprise you, and now is as good a time as any. We're going to visit Sandy."

I should have known. Danny hated surprises. He liked his news delivered without preparations, his birthdays without parties unless he was the first one to know, and his personal life left alone.

He bit his lower lip, unrolled his pack of Luckies from his sleeve, stoked one up and then blew a puff of smoke. If he would have smiled then, I think I would have been in trouble. Instead, he laughed, more to himself, and shrugged his shoulders.

"Boy, am I a jerk. You guys did all this for me and here I am getting ready to get pissed. Gimme a second to get over the shock and I'm gonna let out a yell 'cause I feel so friggin' happy."

Marsha gave him a big kiss and I gave him a good shot in the arm.

"Hey, Marsh," I said as we headed toward Sandy's house, "we did good."

"Yeah, you guys sure did," Danny said. "But tell me what Sandy said when you told her I was coming to see her."

"Well, I hadn't heard from her in over a month, but I wrote last week to tell her we'd be coming up today. I didn't hear from her so I figured everything was cool."

"What if she's out or something?" Danny started to worry.

"Where's she gonna go?" I said, as if I knew. "She's probably waiting by the window for us right now. You'll see."

"Ahhhhhhhh!!!!!!" Danny screamed, then relaxed. "I'm okay, I just got the nerves. Man, I'm getting them bad."

"Ehey, there's nothing to get nervous about," Marsha said, putting her arm around Danny.

Well, as it turned out, Marsha was right. There was absolutely nothing to worry about. In fact, there wasn't even anybody to worry about. When we pulled up in front of Sandy's house we saw a big red and white "SOLD" sign sticking out of the lawn. One look at the house told us it was deserted.

Marsha checked the address on Sandy's letter, but she didn't have to. I knew it was right because everything else felt so wrong. Funny how you know when the whole works are going to blow up in your face. Although I hadn't yet said a word, Danny answered my thoughts.

"Yeah, Sonny, I had a feeling myself. It was too beautiful a day."

GREASE

Marsha knocked at the next door neighbor's and returned with little else than, "She moved away. Friggin' lady wouldn't tell me anything more, except to pull out before she calls the cops."

I was too upset to get upset with a nasty neighbor. We drove home listening to Marsha talking around the radio and a terrible day.

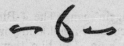

THE ONE THING ABOUT DANNY IS THAT HE'S UNPRE-
dictable. While I was expecting him to hit the bottom
of Heartbreak Lagoon, or stalk the streets at night
like the green slime monster, after he got a good
night's sleep, he returned to the corner kicking up
his heels.

I've always thought it a dangerous thing when people are happy for no apparent reason; strikes me as a
sign of desperation. But this was not the case. Danny
wasn't gunning it, he was just cooled out.

"Hey, Danny-boy, you okay?"

"Well, ol' Sonny-a-mine, I ain't flushed out, but
wrap your ass in a sling and bet it—I'm okay! I mean,
what's-it I'm supposed to do? Sure, I wish Sandy was
up there when we went. Fact, I wish we never went
in the first place. But I blew it from the start with her,
and it's my scene. Sure, I'd like to have her back
beside me, but that ain't the case, and I'm stuck in
this place, so while I'm waitin' for an ace, just let me
feel some lace!"

He was dancing in the street, jumping over dogs,
stopping traffic, as he did a toe-jamb in the middle of
the street. He was blowing out all the bad news from
his heart and head, I suppose, but he was allll-right!

"What say we all make the drive-in tonight?" Danny was jukin' and jivin', snappin' his fingers and whippin' his hips. Our leader was in motion like the ocean.

"Who's all?"

"The whole friggin' gang. The T-Birds and the Ladies. See if your cousin Finn'll lend you his car. Nawh, better yet, invite Finn. Tell him there'll be plenty'a chicks for him to pick from."

"Damn, Danny. That'll bag it for sure!"

A knocked-out summer night. Stars and love in the sky. I was waiting for my cousin Finn on the corner. He blew in like a cool, cool breeze. He had his hair plastered and flipped in the front, his paisley shirt ruffled and winged at the collar, his pants painted on, and his shoes shiny and pointed like a blade. He strolled over, one hand in his pocket hitching up his hips; the other hand, like a swimmer's through water, arced from way out in front of him to around his back. He was pulling himself through the air, stroking with each step. Goddamn if he wasn't every girl's dream.

Finn was one of the few greasers who played sports, and left the jocks faked out of their straps when he was on the field or court. He smoked cigarettes and drank like a demon, but could throw a strike at fifty yards with a football.

On the field, he'd kick off, punt, throw three or four touchdowns a game, return kicks, average around thirty points a game, and at the end of the season he led Rydell High to the city championship, yet he had spent his time on the sidelines practicing his sax. What he was good at, he did perfectly while he was doing it, then completely forget that he had done it at all.

His only frustrations were his musical failings. What he wanted most but could never get was to be a saxman. So he contented himself with an imaginary sax. And truthfully, he played the best goddamn sax you ever seen, if only you could hear it. He could really lay out a nice ballad or bluesy-jazz number like "Take Five." Then he'd get kind of fluid and rotate round his pelvis like his backbone was melting right there in front of you. An actual horn would have taken something away from the total effect.

So, Finn was ready to make the drive-in scene. We whomped down Moyensing Avenue and wheeled up to the Palace, leaning on the horn. Danny and Kenickie and the Ladies were outside ready to go. Rizzo was there waiting nonchalantly on a car outside the Palace. She was surrounded by her Pink Ladies.

Frenchy, Rizzo's best friend, wore white pedal pushers, black shoes, a tight pink sweater and her Pink Ladies jacket. She had her hands dug deeply into the pockets of her jacket, with her collar up, and was cracking gum loud enough to make you draw your piece if you had one. Frenchy had this crazy red hair, actually it was pinkish, that she wore fluffed up and curled under, so the total effect was like a feathered Easter hat. She had dyed her hair so many times that I think it just gave up on her and invented a color all its own. Somehow, she looked kinda good in it. Maybe her caked-on makeup helped some, but she was cute in a hard way. Unreal, but cute. Her goal was to make it to beautician's school. Frenchy had a wise mouth and a heart of gold, but she was a little dumb.

Marty, who had a thing for soldiers, sailors, or just about anything else in a uniform, was really the rose of the Pink Ladies. With her good looks, she could stop a train and make the engineer call in sick. She fashioned herself as a sophisticate, but once she opened her mouth, she blew the image. She was really an innocent.

Marty and Danny were hanging on each other, like they had been for years—Danny running his hand round her ass, Marty combing through the hair on

Danny's chest with her fingers. They were like brother and sister.

Rizzo and Kenickie had their thighs locked together and were making out against the telephone pole. It was a vision of true love.

And Marsha, my peach and lady, had really become one of the Ladies. She sported her PL jacket with pride, over a tight black shirt and slacks, and pink shoes. God, she was beautiful.

We piled into Cousin Finn's Chevy, climbing over each other, fighting over the shotgun seat, and were finally situated when we realized that somebody was missing—Finn.

After checking out the Palace, I found him in the phone booth in the rear. He was forever making phone calls. It seemed like every time he stopped moving, or passed a booth, he'd make a call. There was a real dark mystery surrounding this because Finn never said who he was calling, or who he had called, or even that he had to make a call in the first place. I think he was just addicted to the act of calling people. Maybe he called people he didn't even know. But for a guy who never spoke much, he spent a lot of time on the phone.

"Hey, Cous, ready for take-off?" I asked him through the missing pane of glass in the booth.

Finn nodded and flipped his thumb at me, then hung up without saying good-bye, or another word into the phone. I guess he was a little strange, even if I didn't want to admit it.

With Finn now at the wheel, we copped a U-bie, and whomped down Moymensing Avenue onto Passyunk, heading toward the drive-in. On the way over we stopped at Skippy's Bar and bought a cold case of suds. Skippy did business with us at the back door. While we were stopped we loaded the beer and everybody except me and Finn into the trunk. It was a variation on the ever-popular telephone booth craze. Also, it was a cheap night out.

When we arrived at the Airport Drive-In, Finn and me were alone in the car. I paid for Finn, he insisted. We parked in a spot on the far side so's we could watch the planes taking off if the movie got too bad, which it probably would. The first picture of the triple feature was just starting: "Stock Car Werewolf."

Once we parked, Finn got out and opened the trunk and out came Danny, Rizzo, Marsha, Frenchy, Marty, and Kenickie with the beer.

Finn and Frenchy, me and Marsha were in the front seat. Danny and Marty, Kenickie and Rizzo were in the back. We didn't bother pulling in the speaker since we could hear well enough from those around us, and still be able to talk to each other. The sound track was like an eerie voice from beyond. Kenickie opened beers all around as we cuddled together and tried to pick up on the story . . .

A young, preppy blonde girl was sitting in her professor's office, fidgeting with her purse.

"Professor Bludnick, I think something very strange is happening to Craig."

The professor tried to take it in stride.

"Well, Sharon, boys your brother's age sometimes act very strangely."

He walked around his desk and sat on top of it, facing Sharon, then reached out and put his hand on her shoulder.

"What a snake!" Rizzo yelled.

"Shhhhh!!!" everyone else said, becoming engrossed in this gross flick.

"Professor, you don't understand. Craig has been sneaking out at night, and then returning before sunrise. He's losing sleep and will never be in shape for Saturday's big race . . . and . . . and . . . there's a full moon!!!!!"

"Oh, God!!!" Marsha was scared shitless.

"What crap!" Kenickie groaned.

The professor got up and took Sharon's hand.

"I want to show you something in my lab, dear."

"I don't believe it!" Frenchy yelled. "I've heard some lines but that's the topper!"

Finn was doing finger-bone snaps—a little ditty which involved dislocating the joints in his fingers and then cracking them back into place. He wasn't bored, he just had a short attention span. Frenchy grabbed his hand and wrapped it around her shoulders.

Meanwhile, back in Professor Bludnick's laboratory, cages with half-human, half-ape mutants inside lined the walls. The professor explained:

"Old stock-car drivers, you see. I used to be the track's doctor, Sharon. And these were once all helpless and battered crash victims. Now, look what the miracles of science can do for the lost and brutally ravaged!"

The professor was beaming, with his arms extended toward his cages.

Sharon's eyes bulged.

"AAAAHHHHHHHHHHHHH!!! AAAAAAHHH-HHHHHHHHHH!!!! AAAHHHHHH!!! AAAAHHH-HHHHHHH!!!!!"

Sharon continued to scream.

"Somebody shut that crazy chick up!" Danny yelled.

"So, you think I'm mad?" The professor was looking kindly at Sharon, with murder in his eyes.

Sharon managed to compose herself a bit.

"Oh, oh, no, no, Professor Bludnick."

Sharon backed away.

"Your brother Craig has been coming to visit some of his old friends here in my lab. They live only to see Craig. And he's been getting pointers from them for Saturday's race. So you see, my dear, Craig will not only be ready for the race, but he will win it!"

"What the hell's the full moon got to do with any of this crap?" Marty wanted to know. She was actually trying to piece this thing together.

"All in good time, my dear," Danny told her, imitating Vincent Price while twirling the waxed ends of his mustache.

Professor Bludnick continued:

"But, my radiation technique sometimes has a strange effect when the moon is full."

"There you go, Marty," Danny said.

"What a goddamn bore!" Kenickie said, as he passed another round of suds.

"Hey, Rizz, what's the most embarrassing thing ever happened to you?"

"Hey, Kenick, we gonna talk or watch the movie?"

"I got one other suggestion, Rizz," Kenick sneered.

"Yeah, right, Kenick. You gotta be Jiminy Cricket to get a piece in this crowd."

On the screen, Sharon was screaming again for no apparent reason except maybe the director thought at that point the dialogue was getting pretty thin.

"A'right, who's got their hand on my ass?" Danny asked.

"Oh, sorry, Dan, is that *your* ass?" Kenickie apologized.

"Don't apologize, Kenick. I just thought it was Marty's hand."

"You brute!" Marty said.

"AAAAHHHHHHHH!!! AAAHHHHHHHH!!! AA-AHHHHHHHHHH!!! . . . I CAN'T WATCH ANY MORE OF THIS PICTURE!!!!" Rizzo was standing on the back of the car screaming and pulling her hair and raging like a lady gone mad. She looked beautiful.

Horns blasted from all over the drive-in.

Danny stood up next to Rizzo and yelled, "UP YOURS!" to everyone at the drive-in.

Finn climbed onto the front seat and stood with his

foot on his horn, blaring it rhythmically as he started playing his sax. He fingered the notes on his sax to match those he tooted with his foot on the car's horn. He loved crowds and he was playing to them, trying to make them his.

The place was going crazy. Lights were flashing. People started running in different directions. Horns continued to blare. And Sharon still screamed on the screen and in the background.

Frenchy was drumming on the dashboard with her beer cans, backing up Finn's mean sax. Marsha was squirming around, ducking her head this way and that, trying to keep up with the movie. Kenickie was throwing empty beer cans like hand grenades at the screen. And me, I was adding a back-up vocal of "Doo-wops" to Finn's horn solo. We were going great.

Danny and Marty started dancing to the beeping of the horn, which was sounding more and more like a sax every minute. As Danny and Marty were in the middle of a flip, this enormous jock in a varsity sweater came up with his girlfriend hanging on his arm, munching popcorn.

"A'right, why don't you guys cut the crap, and quick!"

A tough guy. You could tell he tried to fashion himself after Steve Reeves, with his curly golden hair, hard jaw, and clenched fists.

Finn blew a loud sour note right in the jock's face.

"I'm not kidding around with you guys," Jocko said.

"Ehey, there's ladies present," Rizzo said, pointing down at Jocko and his girlfriend.

"Yeah, well, whatever. I ain't gonna tell you again."

This guy was really pushing his luck, and his varsity sweater, to the limit.

Danny clasped his hands to his chest and dropped to his knees.

"Oh my! Oh, my!" he said in a high screechy voice. "Please, a thousand pardons for our lives . . . ya friggin' water buffalo!"

Before anyone knew what had happened, the jock was on his ass. Danny had whipped his feet out from under him and pounced on top of him. In the same motion, Danny pinned the jock's arms and grabbed the box of popcorn from his girlfriend. By the handful, Danny began to stuff the popcorn into the jock's mouth, nose, and ears. His girlfriend starting beating on Danny's back until Rizzo grabbed her from behind and held her.

Me, Finn, and Frenchy continued playing our song, while Marty and Marsha elbowed each other and giggled at the Jock. Jocko was kicking up at Danny, trying to throw him, when Kenickie jumped from the car and landed on Jocko. Kenick unbuckled the jock's pants, assisted by Danny, and together they tore the pants right off him.

"Hey, Finny," Danny yelled, "gun that bitch of yours! I don't know how much longer I can hold this guy down." Danny turned to Jocko. "Want some more popcorn?" Jocko's eyes bulged with anger.

Finn kicked over the engine and torqued it up. We got into the car and waited for Danny and Kenick to jump in so we could make our getaway. Finn was churning dust under his back wheels, ready to cut out.

In a crazy swirl, Danny and Kenickie jumped into the car, leaving the jock in his underwear with his girlfriend standing over him. Finn tore rubber getting out of there. We whomped down an alley of the drive-in, sitting on the back of the car, waving to the audience with Jocko's pants. Danny hooked them over an aerial just before we slipped out the back exit and just as the cops were coming in the front.

As we headed away from the drive-in, we looked back to see Sharon on the screen cheering for her brother in the race. The camera zoomed in for a close-up of the driver and it showed a smiling hairy ape wearing a crash helmet, giving the crowd the "victory" sign with his clawed fingers.

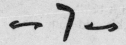

WE DROVE BACK TO THE NEIGHBORHOOD SCREAMING with laughter and singing "Rock Around the Clock." When we were in the clear, the Ladies decided to take us out to eat, since we had taken them to the movies. They were springing for big bucks—Uncle Al's Diner.

Uncle Al's was an all-night spot featuring breakfast at any hour of the day. Danny led us into the back room, a dimly lit cocktail lounge where divorced women and truck drivers hung out. We pushed two tables together and made like we owned the place. By this time, around midnight, we were getting drunk and rowdy.

The waitress came hesitantly to our table. Her name tag read "Tiffany." Sure, like the jewel. She was tired and not really in the mood for us.

"Something from the bar?"

"Now, now, Tiffany," Kenickie said. "You know you can't serve us minors . . . but that's okay." Kenick leaned down and reached under the table. "We brought our own!" He slammed down two six-packs on the table.

Danny said, "The Ladies here are taking us out, so bring us some glasses."

"And some menus, for the ladies," Rizzo added.

Tiffany was confused and intimidated, so she did the easiest thing to do, which was to leave and return with glasses and menus. After we had poured our suds and checked out the menu, Tiffany approached again.

"Okay, what'll it be?"

"Eggs," Kenickie said dully.

"Eggs how?"

"Any style." Kenick didn't look up from the menu.

"Huh?"

"Any style." He smiled at her.

"How do you want your friggin' eggs, mister?" Tiffany was getting testy.

"I want 'em any style. It says right here 'eggs any style,' so that's how I want 'em—any style. Simple enough, right?"

"Shove it!" Tiffany walked away.

"Cheez, I was really gettin' to like her," Kenick said.

Tiffany was back in a second with the manager, a little dark and greasy guy who never made the mob. His suit was wrinkled and too big for him, his hands were shaking, and his eyes were darting around the table from face to face. He was coming apart before our eyes.

"Hey, man, you need a drink," Frenchy said. "C'mon, sit down here beside Frenchy and have a beer." She pulled a chair up to the table. The man was blitzed, completely. He sat.

"Get him a glass," Danny told Tiffany. The manager nodded approval to Tiffany.

Nervously he said, "Tiffany says you were giving her a hard time."

He looked down at his hands, which were twisting around each other.

"Naw, naw, naw," Rizzo said, reassuring him. She had a kind heart for lost causes. "We was just having a little fun, that's all. C'mon, now. Just be cool." Rizzo winked at him.

Tiffany placed a glass in front of the manager.

"Do I take their order?"

"They're okay," the manager said.

"A'right, let's try it again. What'll it be?"

"Eggs," Kenickie said softly.

Tiffany was silent, with her pen poised.

"Eggs . . ." Kenick paused. "Eggs . . . aggerate!"

Rizzo picked up on it instantly.

"Eggs . . . cavate!" she said.

It looked like it was going to go around the table.

"Eggs . . . amine!" Danny snapped.

"Eggs . . . travagant!" Frenchy fired.

Tiffany was being gunned down. It was nothing personal. She was just in the wrong place at the wrong time.

"Eggs . . . pensive!" Marty quipped.

"Eggs . . . ist!" Marsha jumped in.

"Eggs . . . cuse," I said apologetically.

"Eggs . . . haust!" Finn said, revving up.

There was a half second of silence, then the manager said, "Eggs . . . cellent!"

Tiffany stomped away. We whooped and toasted the manager, who was extremely pleased with himself. He smiled and drank to our health.

We introduced ourselves and had a great time drinking with Mike, the manager. We finished off the beers and left a few bucks tip for Tiffany before we split. Mike walked us to the door and yelled after us to be sure and come back soon.

We pulled into the lot behind the Palace, where Rizzo had left her pink Studebaker parked. We split up into two cars—Finn and Frenchy, me and Marsha in Finn's Chevy, and Kenickie and Riz, Danny and Marty in the Stude.

We laughed and talked about the night, then settled

down to making some serious time. Arms, heads, and bodies came together amidst smacking and slurping sounds.

It didn't really matter that both cars were parked next to each other, or that the tops were down on them, or that we were all in plain view of each other, because we weren't doing anything that we hadn't all done on the corner or in front of the Palace—hugging and making out. We knew our limits and when we forgot the Ladies were always there to remind us.

"Let's wait," Marsha told me.

"Let's wait," Frenchy told Finn in the front seat.

"Let's wait," Marty told Danny in the back seat of Rizzo's car.

"Not now," Riz told Kenick.

When we finally broke up for the night, cramped in our backs and with stiff necks, the Ladies went home in Riz's Stude and the guys got a lift with Finn. It couldn't have been a better night if we'd wished or planned for it. We went together like grease and black leather.

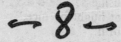

THE LAST FEW WEEKS OF SUMMER WERE UNEVENTFUL. There was really nothing else to do except go back to school, and in a way we were all looking forward to it. But seeing summer go was sad. It was like losing a good friend.

I guess for me, Danny, Roger, and Kenick, there was something special about the summer that had just passed: it was the last summer for each of us before graduating. We didn't know what that meant, but we were sure it meant something, something bad. We heard a lot of talk about all of a sudden growing up and feeling different and being responsible and getting married and having kids and on and on and on. But worst of all, and it pains me to mention it, there was talk of work. A serious respectable position in the world where you had to be every day for most of the rest of your life.

Hell, I didn't want to work, except maybe at Aunt Millie's for a few weeks during the summer. Otherwise, the only things that were important to me was having a girl, being with my friends, getting a set of wheels at some point, and hanging out without anybody getting on my case.

My mother stopped asking me what I wanted to be

when I got out of school. But my father was a little worried. Not because I didn't want to do anything, but because I still considered almost everything a possibility, except college, for his sake.

"What about business?" he'd ask.

"Yeah, Pop, that might be nice."

"Good money in it."

"Yeah, Pop, I think so."

"Then there's always construction. Tough work, but a good future."

"Yeah, Pop, I think so."

"I guess college is out for you, but you could always go to trade school. Television repairs—that's where it's at."

"Yeah, Pop, that might be good."

And so it went. My father would come home every night with another suggestion for my future, and they all sounded to him like golden opportunities. Sometimes I felt like saying, "Yeah, Pop, why don't *you* go build ships down at the Navy Yard and I'll watch the grocery store for you." Maybe I should have told him that I really wouldn't have minded coming into the store with him, but he never suggested it, and I think we would have driven each other crazy anyway. I stopped working for him when I was fourteen 'cause we gave each other the ants. But I had to give it to him, he really cared. He really wanted to see me make something out of myself. More than anything he wanted me to have all the things he never could. How then could I tell him that I didn't want them, in the first place, and that it probably was already too late for me to be anything more than I was?

It's not that I thought for a minute that I would wind up on skid row. That's not me. Basically, when the chips are down, I'm a survivor. So I knew that I would at some point do whatever I had to do to get by. But I also didn't want to pay much attention to it, because one way seemed just as bad as any other to make a living. It wasn't important, and I really didn't care. None of us did. We really couldn't see beyond the corner.

In fact, I don't really remember any of the guys or Ladies ever talking seriously about the future. There really was no future for us. There was tomorrow, and the weekend, and next summer, but no future to put our fingers on.

When we'd talk about what we thought we'd like to do after school was over, it was usually in fun.

"So, my boy, what are you going to do?" Kenick would say, folding his arms across his chest and lifting his chin.

"Do?" Roger asked.

"Yes, son, *do.*"

"Do what?"

"Yes, son, do what."

"Do-what, do-what, do-wop-wop-wop, do-wop do-wop, wop, wop, wop . . ."

And that was usually the end of it.

So, in a way, while this year was a big one for us, we really didn't expect any miraculous developments to arise. One thing at a time was the way to take it. First thing to worry about was whether me, Danny, Roge, and Kenick all had lunch period together. Next thing was to figure a way to get out of gym. After that, a way to get out of classes. So there really was enough to keep me busy without worrying about what I was going to do afterwards. Everything in good time, as my father would say.

Yeah, the summer went, and tonight was the end of it. Tomorrow, Sunday before school, would be worse than tonight. In fact, Sunday was the worst day of my life, and it came every week. I don't even want to talk about it. Suicide-Sunday. Just to play it safe, I tried not to let myself get out of bed.

GREASE

Doody's mother was calling him, which meant that it was exactly nine-thirty, giving the rest of us about another hour to hang on the corner. Usually we would have soaked up every last minute before going home, but we decided to walk Doody to his house and then head home early. Can't avoid the inevitable forever, I guess. Yeah, the summer was over and school was starting, and there was nothing anybody could do about it, except ride with the tide and go with the flow.

"Ehey, Sonny, don't take it so hard," my father said to me when I walked into the house and plopped down on the couch. "Who knows, you might even learn something."

SCHOOL'S IN

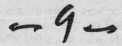

YEAH, BACK AGAIN AT OL' RYDELL, AND FOR THE LAST time, I hoped. The place didn't change much, except it smelled worse than last year. But it was good to see some familiar faces, especially the girls that I never got a chance to follow up on. Every fall it seemed like I was given a shot to redeem myself for all the things I had screwed up the year before. And every fall I started school thinking that this year would be the year to top them all. But every spring, as school was coming to a close, I'd be in the same situation again, just barely getting by.

I was a little early, which was very unusual, so I decided that rather than go right to homeroom, I'd stroll the halls and check things out. There were still a lot of kids hanging around their lockers, sticking up photos or magazine cutouts inside them, putting on locks, or fixing their clothes and combing their hair.

The first day of school was a good day to breeze around. Nobody knew where they were supposed to go, not even the teachers, so nobody really bothered you as long as you looked like you were headed somewhere.

I figured I'd check out the office and see what the schedules looked like, and what teachers I'd have to put up with. There was a crowd of kids around the bulletin board that provided a good cover for me. I mixed into the middle of the crowd and cased the office.

Principal McGee was going over a clipboard in her hand as she leaned on the counter. She was a short, funny-looking lady who wore baby blue Keds with a matching baby blue skirt, a blouse with a Peter Pan collar, and a tight blue sports jacket with brass buttons. Her hair was like straw. Somebody once said that McGee was extremely proud of the fact that she used to be a W.A.C. She looked it.

Teachers were milling around the counter, taking notes and papers out of their mailboxes, talking about their summers in twenty-five words or less, and looking as if they had never left the school during the whole three month break. It was very weird. They looked like they were maybe frozen in motion, back in June, and today somebody thawed them out.

I spotted Mrs. Murdock, who taught Auto Repairs. She was one of my favorite teachers. She was a cute, dark-haired lady who wore a brown jumper with wrenches, screwdrivers, and various other tools sticking out of the pockets.

Mrs. Murdock was talking to Blanche, the school's secretary, who looked more like the car mechanic. She was always covered in mimeo ink and carbon and, like a mechanic, she usually wiped her hands clean on her clothes. Blanche was shuffling through piles of papers on her desk, obviously looking for something that was lost.

"Ahh, here they are!" Blanche said happily.

She handed a stack of papers to Principal McGee.

"Blanche," Principal McGee said, "these are the schedules we never found for spring semester . . . last year. Perhaps next spring we'll find the ones we were supposed to use this semester."

Blanche blushed and went back to rifling through her papers.

Mr. Lynch, who had a strange way of jerking when he walked, something like a toy soldier, was absorbed in his class list. Suddenly, he slapped his hand with the list, and looked up at Mrs. Murdock.

"Ye Gads!" Mr. Lynch yelled. "I've got Kenickie again. He's been here longer than I have!"

I had to cover my mouth to keep from laughing out loud.

It was true, the only other person who had flunked more classes than me was Kenickie, only he flunked even when he went to class.

Mrs. Murdock tried to console Mr. Lynch.

"Don't feel so bad. My homeroom looks like the juvenile court hall of fame."

I wrote down my class schedule and left the office before I had to listen to my name being abused. I was walking back to my locker when I ran into Doody in the hall. We were both checking out our schedules. I couldn't believe it. I slapped my own head without realizing it.

"Hey, Dood. Look-it this! Every teacher I got has flunked me at least once!"

Doody was a pretty straight guy who had a bad habit of always giving advice, whether you wanted it or not.

"Yeah, Sonny," he said, "if you don't watch out you'll be spending all your time in McGee's office."

Well, I had enough of that crap last year.

"Dood, let me tell you, this year she's gonna wish she never seen or heard of me. Mark my words! I'm done getting a lot of cheap crap for nothing!"

Doody got a funny look on his face, and was staring over my shoulder, then he said, "What are you gonna do?"

"What'samatter, you hard of hearing?" I asked him.

"I said I'm done taking crap. I'm not takin' any of McGee's crap and that's that. I don't take crap from anybody!"

Suddenly, from over my shoulder, I heard the high shrieking voice of Principal McGee.

"Sonny!"

To tell the truth, I had a feeling she was behind me from the look on Doody's face before I even opened my mouth. But there was no sense making a big deal out of that now, because it was already too late. Doody, big help that he was, turned from me as if we had never been talking and busied himself in his locker. So there I was faced off with Principal McGee. She lived for moments like this—moments when she'd catch ol' Sonny LaTierri off guard. Yeah, I had a knack of always saying the wrong things at the wrong time. Open mouth, insert foot.

I folded my hands together, reverently, I thought, and looked up at Principal McGee.

"Yes, ma'am?" I said politely.

"Sonny, aren't you supposed to be in class right now?"

"Well, I . . . to tell the truth, ma'am, I was just right now looking at my schedule, and, to be perfectly honest, ma'am, I was a little confused. Maybe you could straighten me out on a few things. You see, I—"

Principal McGee just wasn't gonna go for it.

"So, Mr. LaTierri, you're just dawdling, aren't you? Well, that's a fine way to start the new school year. . . . Are you just going to stand there all day?"

"No, ma'am."

Boy, calling me Mr. LaTierri really said it all. She was definitely in no mood to be charmed. She screwed up her nose, which gave me the feeling she was going to tear into me again.

"And you know what else, Mr. LaTierri? I think it would be a good idea—to develop your school spirit—

if you joined the Clean-Up Committee. You'll meet after school in front of the custodian's office."

"Yes, ma'am. Thank you, ma'am."

Principal McGee walked off down the hall.

Dammit! and shit! I was in school less than an hour and already I was in trouble.

Doody turned back to me and said, "I'm sure glad you didn't take no crap from her, Sonny." Then he knew enough to take off before I stuffed him in his locker.

I was kicking at the floor and the wall of lockers, trying to blow off some steam when along came Eugene. Eugene was one of those guys who it was a real pleasure to hate. Even Eugene seemed to enjoy it. He was duded up in his olive green Robert Hall suit and shiny white bucks. A crowd of guys circled Eugene and spun him around, wiped their fingers over his glasses, and messed up his hair, then just as quickly left him standing in the middle of the hall.

As I walked by Eugene, I couldn't resist scraping my boots over his white bucks. It was mean, I admit, but I got a real pleasure out of it. Eugene looked up at me in disbelief, then from nowhere he pulled out a bottle of shoe polish and did an on-the-spot touch-up on his bucks. He was hopeless.

I had all good intentions of going to class, but I had forgotten to list the room numbers on my schedule. What can you do? I cruised the hall, looking for friends in other classrooms, when Principal McGee's voice came over the P.A. system. She was giving her traditional welcoming speech, which we had heard three years in a row.

"Good morning, boys and girls, and welcome to the start of what will be our greatest year at Rydell . . ."

And so on. I tried to block out her voice, so I could get my thoughts straight. At least as long as McGee was on the P.A. I knew where she was, and she couldn't sneak up on me. Then I had a terrible thought. What if her voice was taped and she was still roaming the halls? I decided to check it out. I cruised the halls close to the walls, taking the turns very cautiously. I peeked into the office and saw Principal McGee seated at her desk behind a microphone reading from some papers. She made some announcements about flu shots and chest X-rays, pep rallies and bonfires, school spirit and the honor roll, and in the middle of a sentence a sneeze began to overtake her. I was laying odds with myself that she wouldn't make it. Her nose was twitching and she was breathing quickly through her mouth. I knew it wouldn't help. Finally, she blew a tremendous sneeze out through her mouth, and it was broadcasted throughout the entire school. The sound of laughter echoed from the classrooms through the deserted hallway.

Principal McGee was undaunted. She continued her spiel.

"Now, for some major economic news. School lunches have been promoted from 25¢ to 35¢. Sorry, kids. Yearbook pictures to $2.50 a set. And senior class rings have graduated from $25 to $35. A word of caution here! Several of last year's seniors have been offering cut-rate buys on their used rings. If any of you are rash enough to try and economize in this manner, remember, you'll go through life with the wrong year on your finger."

Oh, horrors! Boy, I swear, sometimes I think you have to be a little senile to become a principal.

There was no stopping ol' McGee.

"And now, boys and girls, for the really good news, and probably one of the most exciting things ever to happen to Rydell High . . . The National Bandstand Television Show has selected Rydell as a representative American high school and will do a live telecast from our very own gym with winners in the National

Dance-off! This is the first time in National Bandstand's history they've left the studios for a location show. Now, this is our chance to show the entire nation what fine, bright, clean-cut, wholesome youth we have here at Rydell . . ."

Principal McGee was finally winding up her speech.

"And, in closing, I would like to say to all students on this, the first day of a new school year, we, the faculty, are here to help you. And if you need us at any time, feel free. Remember, you've not only got a 'prince' in principal, but there's a 'pal' there, too."

Uggh!

Over in Auto Repairs the kids were going wild, jumping up and down and cheering for the end of McGee's speech. Mrs. Murdock, who was reading a book, did not even look up, but instead gave a ridiculously loud blast on a whistle that hung around her neck. The room fell silent, leaving most of the kids with their hands over their ears.

"This year, boys, I mean business!"

She returned to reading her book.

I spent the rest of the morning cruising the halls, and decided that I'd meet the T-Birds for lunch, then try to make afternoon classes, depending on how I felt.

Doody, Roge, and Putzie were hanging out on the back steps eating their lunches. Doody grabbed my lunch bag out of my hand.

"Ehey, Dood, I'm gonna cream ya if you don't give me back my lunch."

Doody tossed my lunch over to Roger. They wanted to play games.

"Listen, Sonny," Doody said, "I'm doin' it for your own good. You're not supposed to eat that, you're supposed to bury it."

"C'mon, shitheads, that's a homemade lunch."

"You mean your old lady dragged her ass outta bed for you?" Putzie asked.

"Yeah, well, she does it every year on the first day of school," Doody explained for me.

"Hey, Dood, enough!"

He was cruisin' for a bruisin'.

I finally snagged my lunch out of the air as it sailed over my head. I checked for damage, but it looked okay. Kenickie came up and looked over my shoulder into the bag.

"Hey, Sonny, what did ya do with the rest of him?"

"Who?"

"Whoever ya got in that bag, you shouldn't have saved the small chunks. They got ways of tracing things like that."

"Yooh, Kenick! Where you been all summer?" Putzie broke in excitedly.

"What are you, my mother?"

"I was just asking."

Kenick rolled his collar and leaned against the railing.

"Well, I been hanging out with these guys, and working a little bit."

"Working?" Putzie couldn't believe it.

"That's right, moron. I was luggin' boxes at Bargain City."

"Hey, nice job, Kenick," Putzie said.

"Ehey, Putzie! Eat me! I'm saving up to buy some wheels."

Putzie stood up and approached Kenick.

"You wanna hear what I did this summer?"

"No." Kenick sat on the steps and looked around the schoolyard.

Danny was across the yard facing a wall, leaning on one hand, with a knocked-out looking girl between him and the wall. As he was talking he was running his other hand around her ass. The girl was giggling, enjoying it immensely.

"Hey, Zuko!" Kenickie called across to Danny.

Danny turned from the girl slowly, and smiled over to us guys on the steps. He pinched the girl playfully on the ass and came over.

"How's it hanging?" Danny was looking cool.

"See any new broads over there, Danny?" Kenick wanted a report.

"Naw. Nothing. Just the same old chicks everybody's already made it with."

Danny was doing a number on Putzie. Putzie was really impressed with the T-Birds, and especially with Danny. He had been trying for years to get in the gang.

"What'd you do all summer, Danny?" Putzie was taking a poll I think.

"I been hanging out and what not . . . you know what I mean?"

"Yeah, I know what you mean. It's tough with all those chicks hanging around, ain't it Danny? They just won't leave you alone." Putzie was trying to make a case for himself again by sucking up to Danny.

"Ahh, Putzie," Kenick said, "the only thing that won't let you alone are the flies."

"So, how was the action this summer, Danny?" Putzie didn't miss a beat.

"Flippin'. I met one chick who was sort of cool."

"You mean she puts out?" Putzie asked.

"Is that all you ever think about?"

"Friggin' A!"

Danny was getting bored. He ignored Putzie.

"Hey, Sonny," he said to me, "who you got for English?"

"I got Old Lady Berger again. She hates my guts."

"Naw, she's got the hots for ya, Sonny. That's why

she keeps puttin' ya back in her class." Danny laughed.

"Yeah, Sonny," Kenick chimed in, "she's just waitin' for ya to grow up."

"Hey, Kenick, stuff it!"

Danny stretched out his arms, then reached back and brought out his comb and stroked it through his hair.

"What say we take a walk over to the football field and have a look at practice?" Danny asked.

Putzie was the first to yell, "Yeah, yeah, great idea, Danny!"

Kenickie got up and walked next to Danny, with Doody at his side. I decided to check the action in the lunch room.

"See you guys later," I called after them.

"Right." "Right." "Right."

Putzie was trailing the T-Birds, trying to catch up to Danny. I heard him saying to Danny, "Her knockers, Danny! Tell me about her knockers!"

~ 10 ~

FRIDAY NIGHT WE ALL PLANNED TO MEET AT THE PEP rally and see what was happening. A bonfire was going behind the bleachers and a dummy of a Gladiator, the team we were playing, was burning on top of the fire. There was a pretty good crowd on hand at the field.

Me, Doody and Roger were cruising, checking out the cheerleaders. They were a sweet looking crew, especially when they jumped up and landed before their skirts came down. Ahhh, a vision of pure beauty! They were really spirited, clapping and chanting all of the old Rydell cheers in rhythm. It was almost enough to make you wanna play.

We ran onto the field in front of the cheerleaders and held each other's hands, and did our version of the Rydell cheer for the cheerleaders:

"Do a split, Do a yell, Shake a tit, For old Rydell!"

We cut out off the field and strolled around behind the bleachers, looking for action. We found Danny leaning against the stands smoking a Luckie. He was just hanging out casing the scene.

"Seen Kenick?" Danny asked, rolling up his T-shirt sleeves.

"Nope," Doody said, imitating Danny.

"He'll be around," I said. "He called me and said he had a surprise for us tonight."

Just then, we heard the strangest noise coming from behind us. We turned to see a pair of crooked headlights coming across the field. It looked like a car but sounded like a meat grinder. It was wheezing and choking, burning and gagging. Then into the light from the bonfire and the field came a monstrous, battered-up old convertible, dated somewhere in the late-forties or early-fifties. Its make was hard to figure. Behind the wheel, with a smile from ear to ear and waving over the hood (the windshield was missing) was Kenickie.

The car never actually came to a stop; it just kind of wound down. Kenickie was beaming with pride as he opened the door and got out. The door creaked loudly and slipped from the hinge to hang down at an angle. Without losing his smile, Kenickie gave the door a yank and lifted it back into place.

"Well . . ." Kenick said, circling the demon car. "Whadda ya think?"

We came up to the car, but I think everyone was a little afraid to get too close.

"What the hell is it, Kenick?" I asked.

"It's a hunk of junk!" Danny said.

Kenick got offended.

"Yeah, well, just wait 'til I give it a paint job and soup up the engine. She'll run like a champ. I'm racing her at Thunder Road."

"Thunder Road?" Doody yelled, laughing.

"Yeah! You wanna make something of it?"

"Ehey, Kenick, I wanna see you make something of that heap," I said.

We were trying to figure out whether Kenick's car would ever move again when we heard a tremendous roar of a big, mean machine coming down upon us. We looked up to see a black hot rod with red flames along its side spelling out "Hell's Chariot." It was a fierce looking set of wheels. The car circled nearby, and slowed to almost a stop. I recognized the driver as Leo, the leader of the Scorpions. He had some of his gang with him hanging out the windows showing the scorpions on the sleeves of their jackets.

Instinctively we banded together shoulder to shoulder, and stared like mean and ugly killers right into their faces.

"Hey, whadda the Scorpions doin' here? This ain't their territory," I said without taking my eyes off the guy in the back seat.

"Think they want to rumble?" Kenick asked, throwing out his chin.

"Yeah, well, if they do, we'll be ready." Danny gave the word we needed for backup.

Hell's Chariot cruised by the bonfire and crawled up to where Kenick had parked his shitwagon. The Scorpions were all hanging out the window trying to stare us down. Nobody made a move. Suddenly, Hell's Chariot spun around in the lot and laid rubber wheeling away and out of sight.

We were all a little bit shaken up, but nobody, of course, was ready to admit it. Kenickie picked up where he had left off as if nothing had happened.

"Yeah, this car is going to be Make-Out City . . ."

"A chick's got to be willing to go three-quarters of the way before she can even get in it, huh, Kenick?" Roger said.

"Let me tell you," Kenick said, walking around his car. "I'm gonna have me overhead lifters and four-barrel quads, a fuel-injection cut-off and chrome-plated rods."

He was snapping his fingers and shaking his hips as he circled his car, laying his jive on us.

"Yeah, with a four-speed on the floor, the chicks'll

be waitin' at the door. It ain't no shit, ya know, I'll be gettin' lots of tit, in my Greased Lightnin'.''

Kenick ran his hand along the front fender, talking to his car.

"Yeah, Greased Lightnin', you're burnin' up the quarter mile. Go, Greased Lightnin', you're coastin' through the heat-lap trials. Greased Lightnin', you are supreme. The chicks are gonna cream for Greased Lightnin'.''

We were snapping our fingers in rhythm to Kenick's jukin'. He was going great.

"I'll have me purple frenched taillights and thirty-two inch fins—a palomino dashboard and dual muffler twins.''

Kenick jumped onto the trunk of the car, and tight-rope walked toward the front.

"With new pistons, plugs, and shocks, I'm gonna get off my rocks. Ya know that I ain't braggin', but she's a real pussy wagon, my Greased Lightnin'.''

He jumped down and landed in front of us. We whooped and cheered. Kenickie leaned back onto the grill of Greased Lightnin', flipped up his collar, and smiled like the cute little kid he must have been ten years ago.

"What, Kenickie? You got nothin' to do but walk around on top of a junked car?" It was Rizzo. She was coming from behind the bleachers with the Pink Ladies.

"Oh, Zuko? There you are Danny-boy . . . we got a surprise for you. C'mere.''

Danny strode over to where Rizzo and the Pink Ladies were standing beside the bleachers, and when he got there Rizzo stepped aside. Standing behind her was Sandy. Neither of them could believe it.

Sandy looked as lovely as she had during the summer, and still wore a dress that looked like it belonged in Catholic school.

"Danny?" she said, kind of bewildered.

Danny nearly jumped in his boots when he heard her voice. I guess he really didn't believe it was her until she spoke.

"Sandy? Wow! This is too much! It's cra-azy!"

Sandy let out a little giggle.

"I don't believe it, Danny Zuko."

"I don't believe it either, Sandy Ollson. What are you doing at Rydell?"

"I go to school here. We moved here over the summer."

The Pink Ladies and the T-Birds watched their reunion with amusement. Danny rushed toward Sandy, but just before he reached her he stopped dead in his tracks and looked from Sandy back to the T-Birds behind him. He had completely lost his cool and I think he realized it, because in the next second he shook back his shoulders, flipped his hair, and dug his hands into his pockets. Back to Mr. Cool, The Iceman.

"But that's cool, baby, cool. You know how it is . . ." Danny was laying the T-Bird rap on her, which she had never really heard or seen in action before.

Sandy looked at Danny as if he had gone a little nuts.

"Danny!"

"Hey, I said, it's cool . . . you know . . . cool. Real cool." He looked over his shoulder to Kenick, Roger and Doody.

"Danny, what's the matter with you?" she asked.

Danny nodded to the T-Birds, saying with a flip of his head that she was just another one of the chicks chasin' his case. I couldn't believe how badly he was blowin' it.

"Whaddah ya mean, what'samatter with me? What'samatter with you, baby?" Danny pulled his pack of Luckies out from his shirt sleeve and lit one up.

"What happened to the Danny Zuko I met at the shore?"

Sandy looked like she might be getting ready to cry.

"Whaddah I know? Maybe there's two of us. Was he short? Was he tall?" Danny dragged on his smoke, and leaned back on his heels.

"Listen," he told Sandy, "that don't give me much to go on. Look in the Yellow Pages. . . . Take out a Want-Ad. . . . Try Missing Persons. . . ."

The T-Birds got a laugh out of that.

"Danny Zuko, you're a fake and a phony and I wish I'd never laid eyes on you!"

Sandy turned away and took off across the parking lot. I started to walk over to Marsha, but she gave me about the meanest ugliest look I had ever seen, then stomped off after Sandy. Great, now she was going to be pissed at me because Danny was a shithead.

The T-Birds jumped into Kenickie's car as Kenick said, "Yeah, Danny, you don't need her. You don't need nobody. Let's get the suds!"

I walked around to Danny's side of the car and looked at him.

"Get in, Sonny, and don't give me no crap," was all he said.

— 11 —

BY THE END OF THE FIRST WEEK AT SCHOOL I HAD MAN-
aged to get caught skipping only two classes, gym and
English. When I got called into McGee's office for
missing gym, I limped, so she really couldn't do anything except send me to the infirmary, which I knew
she didn't want to do in case there was really something wrong with my ankle, which would mean that I'd
milk the injury for all it was worth once it was official.

But when I got called in for missing English class,
she gave me time in detention. I had missed English
the very first day of school, but she didn't know that.
It was the second English class I missed that she was
concerned with. Now, the reason I skipped the second
class was because I had missed the assignment given
out in the first class. So, since I wasn't prepared for
the second class, I skipped it. That's what tends to
happen when you skip classes. It snowballs on you. It
pays to skip them all once you start, 'cause you won't
know what's happening anyway, if you do show up
later. But that wasn't the kind of explanation I could
very well lay on Principal McGee, so I just told her
that my ankle was hurting too much for me to be able
to think about words. She said she understood the

71

problem, at least in my case, then gave me a detention slip.

I was sitting in Detention Room, thinking that it wasn't really that bad a thing. Detention cut in on your free time, but it was a good place to catch up on your thinking and sleep. The Detention Room was deserted. It was too early in the school year for anybody except me to be in it. Principal McGee hadn't even assigned a monitor to watch the room yet. But there I was, doing my time. I suppose I could have cut out, since there was no one who would be the wiser, but I felt like I had to pay my dues for skipping English class, so that the next time I cut I could do it with a clear conscience.

I started to nod out when the door opened and Marsha peeked in. It was great to see her. She hadn't spoken to me since Danny put down Sandy in front of the T-Birds and Ladies.

"Hiya, Sonny. Doin' time, huh?"

Marsha walked in with her books held over her boobs and sat beside me.

"Yeah, I was sittin' here, just sittin' here, thinkin' about my sins and wondering if I'm ever gonna wise up. How's by you? Lookin' good . . . lookin' real good."

Marsh smiled shyly.

"Thanks, Sonny. Doin' okay. Been thinking about you and me and I decided it was dumb of me to get pissy with you because of Danny, that jerk. I don't understand men, that's all. Men are rats. Worse. Fleas on rats. Worse than that. Amoebas on fleas on rats. Too low for dogs to bite. But you're alright, Sonny. Sometimes you talk too much and don't say a whole lot, but you're okay, really."

"Hey, Marsh, don't stop now, flattery'll get you everywhere. You're giving me a hard head."

"Cut it out."

Marsha was alright herself. She was a good one, really.

"So what's been happening? I mean, how's Sandy taking it?"

"Well, it's hard to say. I think she's more confused than anything. You know there's a lot she doesn't understand. And the T-Birds and Ladies are a very strange breed to her. I think she's never seen anything quite like us. And that number Danny laid on her, first being Mr. All-American at the shore, then acting like a big jerk, trying to be cool in front of his friends. I don't think she really knows what's happening."

"Yeah, I know what you mean. Danny refuses to talk about it."

I want to reach out and hold Marsha's hand, but there was no way I could really get to her without climbing all over myself and looking like a jerk, so I just kind of stretched my hand out on my desk hoping she would get the hint. Something happened to me when I looked at her, especially at her eyes. She had these crystal blue eyes that had a way of taking you right into them. I had to fight with myself not to look her in the eyes. As I was struggling with myself, she touched my hand and I couldn't help looking up at her and smiling. She had a way of knowing just what I meant when I couldn't say it.

She was so nice and so pretty and about the best girl I had ever met, and I wanted nothing more than to tell her all that, but I couldn't. I just couldn't. Whenever I even thought about it my throat would go dry and I'd get the nerves, bad. I don't even know what the big deal was, but there was something about telling a girl how you felt about her that kept you from doing it.

So we were sitting there just barely touching hands, fingertips really, and I decided that one of these days I was going to tell Marsha exactly what she meant to me, one of these days real soon. Who knows, maybe I'd be the first of the T-Birds to have a steady. I know we were all looking for one, but nobody wanted to admit it, and everybody was scared to be the first one to do it. But Marsh was the kind of girl who'd make a great steady, and I didn't want her to get away from me.

Marsha broke the silence.

"We had a pajama party Saturday night over at Frenchy's house. It was me, Rizzo, Jan, Sandy, and yeah, Frenchy."

"How'd it go?"

"Kinda weird. Wanna hear?"

"Sure."

Marsha started telling me about her night at Frenchy's . . .

~ 12 ~

. . . WE WERE HANGING AROUND FRENCHY'S ROOM IN
our baby dolls, mules and curlers, putting on and tak-
ing off makeup, reading magazines, and trading dirty
jokes. You know, the usual stuff.

Rizzo had smuggled a bottle of wine past Frenchy's
mom, and she was filling up some jelly glasses that
Frenchy had stashed in her bedroom. We had the TV
on with the sound off, and the radio goin', listenin' to
Vince Fontaine.

Ol' Vince was layin' his usual rap—"Hey, hey, hey, this
is the main brain, Vince Fontaine, at Big Fifteen! Spinnin'
the stacks of wax, here at the house of Wax—W-A-X-X
on your dial! Cruisin' time, 10:30. Sharpshooter pick hit
of the week—a brand-new one shootin' up the charts like
a rocket by the Vel-doo Rays—goin' out to Ronnie
and Shirley, the kids down at Wagner's Ballroom, and
especially to all you young lovers—listen in while I give
it a spin!"

Jan was watching the picture on television.

"Hey, you guys, look at what Loretta Young is
wearing."

"Yuck!" Rizzo stuck out her tongue. "I can't stand
her. I keep waiting for her to get her dress caught in the
door. Hey, Frenchy, throw me a ciggie-butt, willya?"

"Yeah, me too while you got the pack out," I said.

Frenchy asked Sandy if she wanted one. . . . Sandy got this funny look on her face.

"Oh, no thanks," she said. *"I don't smoke."*

"Ahh, go on, try it," Rizzo said. *"It ain't gonna kill ya. Give her a Hit Parade."*

Frenchy lit up a cigarette and handed it to Sandy. Sandy looked at it nervously, then wrapped her lips around it and sucked in. Her eyes bugged out, then she turned green and started coughing.

Rizzo slapped her on the shoulder.

"Sandy, I shoulda told ya, don't inhale if you're not used to it."

Frenchy came over to Sandy to explain how to smoke.

"Look, I'll show you how to French inhale. It's really cool. Watch."

Frenchy took a long, hard haul on the cigarette and let the smoke slip up into her nostrils.

"Uggh!" Jan yelled. *"That's the ugliest thing I ever saw!"*

"What are ya kiddin' me?" French said proudly. *"The guys go crazy over that. That's how I got my nickname, Frenchy."*

"Yeah, sure it is. Tell me another one," Rizzo said.

Jan picked up the bottle of wine that Rizzo had snuck in and she inspected the label.

"Wow, Riz, Italian Swiss Colony. It's imported. Hey, I brought some Twinkies, anybody want one?"

"Twinkies and wine? That's real class, Jan," I said.

"Yeah, well, don't be such a smart-ass, Marsha. It says right here that it's a dessert wine!"

"Don't forget Sandy," Rizzo said, taking the wine and handing it to Sandy. *"You didn't get any wine."*

"Oh, that's okay . . . no, thanks." Sandy seemed a little embarrassed that Rizzo was putting her on the spot.

"Hey, I'll bet you never had a drink before . . ." Rizzo called her out.

"Sure I did . . . I had some champagne at my cousin's wedding." Sandy acted more sure of herself then.

"Oh, ring-a-ding-ding!" Rizzo twirled her finger in the air, then handed the bottle to Sandy while standing over her.

Sandy took a small sip from the bottle.

"Ahhh, naw, naw, naw. That ain't the way," Rizzo said, taking back the bottle. "Ya gotta chug it. Like this!"

Rizzo tilted her head back with the bottle in her mouth and downed a big slug of wine.

Jan put her two cents in.

"Yeah, the only way to drink wine is to chug it, Sandy. Otherwise you swallow air bubbles and that's what makes you throw up."

"I never knew that, Jan," I said.

"Well, it's true. Rudy from the Capri Lounge told me the same thing one night."

Rizzo handed the bottle back to Sandy and bravely she took another shot at the bottle, this time taking a bigger swig of wine and almost choking to death getting it past her throat. But once it was down, she managed a smile.

"Hey, Sandy, you ever wear earrings? I think they might keep your face from lookin' so skinny."

Jan was standing over Sandy now, holding her face in her hands.

"C'mere, Frenchy. Take a look, see what you think."

"Ya know, it's true, Sandy," Frenchy told her. "Would ya like me to pierce your ears for ya? I'm gonna be a beautician, y'know."

Sandy swallowed hard and looked pretty nervous.

"Oh, no thanks. I don't think so . . . my father'd probably kill me."

"What? You still worry about what your old man thinks?" Rizzo asked.

77

"Well . . ." Sandy thought it over. *"No. But isn't it awfully dangerous?"*

Rizzo leaned down over Sandy.

"You ain't afraid are ya?"

Sandy snapped back proudly, *"Of course not!"*

"Good," Frenchy said.

"Here, Frenchy," Jan said. She reached for her Pink Ladies jacket, took her circle pin off and handed it to Frenchy. *"You can use my virgin pin."*

"Ehey," Rizzo said, *"it's nice to know it's good for something."*

"What's that supposed to mean?"

"Nothin', Jan, nothin', I was just teasin'."

Frenchy took Sandy by the hand.

"C'mon, Sandy, let's go in the john. My mother'll kill me if we get blood all over this rug."

"Huh?" Sandy looked at Frenchy.

"Ahh, it only bleeds for a second. Come on."

Sandy turned a little pale.

"Listen, I'm not feeling too well . . . I . . ."

Rizzo put her arm around Sandy.

"Don't worry, Sandy. If she screws up, she can always fix your hair so your ears don't show."

Frenchy led Sandy into the bathroom. We sat around drinking wine and checking out our complexions. Suddenly, there was a yell from the bathroom. It was Sandy. We heard Frenchy telling her, *"Sandy, Sandy, come on now. Beauty is pain!"* Frenchy stuck her head out of the bathroom and said, *"Hey, Jan, get me some ice cubes to numb Sandy's earlobes."*

"Ahh, just let the cold water run awhile and then stick her ear under it," Jan said without looking up from her magazine.

Just then, an awful gagging sound came from the bathroom. Frenchy came out with a puzzled look on her face and her arms spread open.

"I don't get it," she said. "Sandy's sick. I did one ear and she saw the blood and that was it—BLOUGH!!"

Frenchy sat on the floor, in the middle of the girls. Jan was watching her wiping the blood from her fingers with a tissue.

"Frenchy, you're not gettin' your hands on my ears," Jan told her.

"Yeah, well, you'll be sorry, Jan. I been accepted at the La-Cafury Beauty School."

"You dropped outta Rydell?" None of us could believe it.

Frenchy took it in stride.

"I don't look at it as dropping out. I see it as a very strategic career move. Just wait until I'm a very famous hair-stylist."

Frenchy was primping her pinkish-red locks in the mirror.

Sandy called out from the bathroom, "Frenchy, it's starting to bleed again. I'm sorry, but it is."

Frenchy rose and went to the bathroom.

"Miss Goody-Two-Shoes makes me wanta barf," Rizzo said, making a face in the direction of the bathroom. Rizzo walked around the bedroom, holding her head up, with her hands folded together, doing an imitation of Sandy for us girls.

"Look at me, I'm Sandra Dee, lousy with virginity. I won't go to bed till I'm legally wed. I can't, I'm Sandra Dee."

Riz started skipping around the room.

"Watch it, hey, I'm Doris Day, I wasn't brought up that way." Riz waved her finger at us. "I won't come across, even Rock Hudson lost his heart to Doris Day."

Riz bent over and put her hands on her knees, and rocked on them, swinging her ass.

"I don't drink or swear, I don't rat my hair, I get ill from one cigarette. Keep your filthy paws off my silky drawers. Would you pull that stuff with Annette?"

She was having a great time, and doin' a pretty good impression of Sandy.

"As for you, Troy Donahue, I know what you wanna do. You got your crust, I'm no object of lust— I'm just plain Sandra Dee."

Riz continued to jive.

"No, no, no, Sal Mineo! I would never stoop so low! Please keep your cool, now you're starting to drool . . . Fongool! I'm Sandra Dee!"

Rizzo folded down on her knees laughing, and we laughed along with her until we looked up and saw Sandy standing in the bedroom, looking teary-eyed.

Sandy looked down at Rizzo. "Who do you think you are—making fun of me?!!" Sandy ran out of the bedroom crying. . . .

. . . "So, Marsha," I said, "what finally happened?"

Marsh looked kind of faraway.

"Well, Sonny, I think Rizzo apologized to Sandy, but that didn't help Sandy's feelings any, you know? I just think she's really confused, and still is pretty crazy about Danny. That thing with Rizzo'll blow over, but I don't know about Danny. Sandy said she couldn't see what she ever saw in Danny Zuko at the start. She said he was just like all the others."

"Well, she'll get over it. What say we cut out of here and go to the Palace for something to eat?"

"What about your detention time, Sonny?"

"I been detained too long already! Shall we?"

I left school with Marsha on my arm, but from time to time I sneaked a peek over my shoulder lookin' for McGee, and just knowing that somewhere behind one of those windows she was just waiting and watching. She knew, and I knew, that all she had to do was look out for me long enough and eventually she was bound to catch me screwing up. The odds were definitely on her side.

— 13 —

ME, DANNY, AND ROGER WERE CRUISING THE BACK streets, stripping parts from parked cars as a present for Kenickie's Greased Lightnin'. We got four baby moons from a Chevy, a chrome mirror from a Chrysler, and a pair of big sponge dice from a black Buick. Roger copped an aerial from a big-ass Caddie, but decided to keep it for himself as a weapon.

Leo and the Scorpions had us all a little on edge since our run-in with them at the bonfire, so we kept one eye peeled in case they tried to sucker us from behind. In the meantime, we were collecting weapons for ourselves, getting ready in case the Scorpions called us out. We weren't really fighters. In fact we prided ourselves on being lovers, and fleet-footed runners. In all the time I was in the T-Birds, which was from the beginning, we were never in a gang fight. We just gave everybody the impression that we spent most of our time kicking ass, so nobody screwed around with us. But it was no lie, we were never in a big fight. Now, all of a sudden, I found myself working on a zip-gun in Machine Shop, and I wasn't doing so good on it, 'cause I didn't know the first thing about a gun and I couldn't even ask anybody for help. I wasn't even sure if it would work, but I figured as long as it looked like a gun, it would amount to the same thing. I really wasn't about to shoot anybody. I just figured I could get some nice results without ever having to fire it. But lately things had been pretty quiet, almost too quiet.

We stopped by Skippy's and picked up some beer, then headed for the corner with the suds and our take for the night. Kenickie was waiting for us, behind the wheel of Greased Lightnin'. He had his legs stretched out on the dashboard, with his back leaned against the door. He looked like he was getting ready to fall asleep.

"Yooh, Kenick!" I yelled. "We got presents for you."

"Yeah," Danny said. "Open your mouth and close your eyes."

"Heh, not in your life!" Kenick said, sitting up.

We gathered around the car with our hands behind our backs. In turn we put the mirror, hubs, and dice on the hood of the car.

"Christ!" Kenick jumped out of the car. He looked carefully at each of the items.

"Hey, you guys," he said, "these hubcaps ain't got a scratch on 'em. They must be worth two beans apiece, easy."

"Kenick," Roger said, "we ain't givin' 'em to you to sell, shithead. They're for Greased Lightnin'. We figured since we're all gonna be knockin' off a piece at one time or another in her, we felt like we'd chip in and help you fix her up."

"Ahh, cheez, fellas . . . I'm touched. Really. This moves me beyond words." Kenick shrugged his shoulders and rolled his head from side to side. "What can I say? . . . Me and Greased Lightnin' are truly humiliated, and we both thank you guys from the bottom."

We each grabbed a hubcap and slapped it on a wheel, while Kenickie hung the dice on the door, since he didn't have a windshield, or a rear-view mirror. One thing at a time. A windshield wasn't going to be an easy take. It required some planning. A little engineering, to say the least. Kenick put the mirror in his glove compartment until he had a windshield to put it on.

We were standing back admiring our work when we heard a siren in the distance. That meant either one of two things—either the cops were going to collect money, or somebody had discovered parts of their car missing. We jumped into Greased Lightnin' and took off.

Lunch was over and me and Danny had just finished eating our sandwiches in the bleachers at the
football field. We were walking around the track when
we caught sight of the girls practicing their cheerleading across the field. We strolled over and noticed that
Sandy was among them.

Sandy looked past Danny and smiled at me.

"Hiya, Sonny. Things must be pretty bad if the company you keep is any indication of how things are
going."

"Hey, Sandy, how's by you?" I said, laughing. It
was a pretty funny line. Danny didn't think so.

Danny approached Sandy, and I stepped away
from them.

"Hiya, Sandy," he said shyly.

Sandy turned her head from him and exposed a big
Band-Aid on her ear.

"Hey, what happened to your ear?" Danny asked.

"Huh? . . . Oh, nothing. Just an accident." Sandy
put her hand over her ear.

"Hey look, Sandy, uh, I hope you're not bugged
about that first day at school. I mean, couldn't ya tell
I was glad to see you?" Danny stuck his hands into his
leather and kicked lightly at the ground with his feet.

"Well, you could've been a little nicer to me in front of your friends, you know."

"Ahh, Sandy, you don't know those guys. They just see ya talkin' to a chick and right away they think she puts out . . . well, you know what I mean."

Sandy looked a little confused.

"I'm not sure, Danny. It looked to me like maybe you had a new girlfriend or something."

Danny perked up.

"Are you kiddin'! Listen, if it was up to me, I'd never even look at any other chick but you."

Sandy started to blush.

"Hey, Sandy, tell ya what. We're throwin' a party in the park later for Frenchy. She's gonna quit school before she flunks out, and go to beauty school. How-dja like to make it on down there with me?"

Sandy thought about it for a second.

"Yeah, I'd really like to, Danny, but I'm not so sure those girls want me around anymore."

"Ahh, listen, nobody's gonna start gettin' salty with you when I'm around. Uh-uhh!"

Sandy broke into a big smile.

"All right, Danny. As long as you're with me. Let's not let anyone come between us again. Okay?"

Just then Patty Simcox came rushing up with a baton in her hand, wearing her cheerleader's outfit.

"Oh, hiiiiii Danny! Don't let me interrupt."

Patty handed the baton to Sandy.

"Here, Sandy, why don't you twirl this for a while."

Patty put her arm around Danny and took him to one side.

"I've been dying to tell you something, Danny. You know what I found out after you left my house the other night? My mother thinks you're cute."

Patty turned toward Sandy and said over her shoulder, "He's such a lady killer."

Sandy slapped her hand with the baton and said

sharply, "Isn't he though!" Sandy may have been hurt, but she didn't show it.

Well, it looked to me like Danny had gotten busted, right there in front of Sandy.

"What were you doing at her house?" Sandy asked Danny.

"Ah, come on, I was just copying down some homework."

"Sandy," Patty said, taking her arm, "I think we should practice."

"Yeah, let's! I'm just dying to make a good impression on all those cute lettermen." Sandy looked across the field where the team was gathering for practice.

"Oh, so that's why you're wearing that stupid outfit—you're gettin' ready to show off your skivvies to a bunch of horny jocks!" Danny was steamed.

"Don't tell me you're jealous, Danny Zuko."

Sandy was cooled out.

"What? Of that bunch of meatheads! Ha! Don't make me laugh. Ha! Ha!"

"Just because they can do something you can't do?" Sandy was rubbing it in.

"Yeah, sure, right," Danny said, getting nervous.

"Okay, Mr. Big-mouth, what have you ever done?"

Danny turned on Patty and screamed, "Stop twirling that stupid baton, willya?" Then he turned back to Sandy and was stuck for a moment. "Well, ahh, oh yeah! I won a hully-gully contest at the 'Teen-Talent' record hop."

"Ahhh, Zuko, you don't even know what I'm talking about." Sandy was getting to Danny, but good.

"Whaddaya mean? Look, I could run circles around those jerks."

"But you'd rather spend your time copying other people's homework."

"All right, wisemouth, the next time they have tryouts for any of those teams, I'll show you what I can do."

Danny thought he had finally won out, until Patty opened her mouth.

"Oh, Danny, what a lucky coincidence! Team tryouts are on Monday!"

I think Danny wanted to strangle her, but instead he said, "Okay, I'll be there."

"Sure. Big talk," Sandy said.

"You think so, huh. Hey, Patty, whendja say those tryouts were?"

"Monday, tenth period."

"Good, I'll be there. You're gonna come watch me, aren't you, Patty?"

I guess Danny was putting in his digs now.

"Ohhhh, ohhhh, I can't wait!"

Sandy walked away from Danny and Patty.

"Solid," Danny said to Patty. "I'll see ya there, sexy."

"Ohh, toodles!" Patty chirped, chasing after Sandy. "I'm so excited!"

"Come on, Patty, let's practice," was all Sandy said.

Danny and me were walking off the field together.

"Well, pal-a-mine," I said to him, "looks like you really did it this time, huh? I mean, you not only screwed up with Sandy again, but you got yourself wired into team tryouts. When's the last time you ran except to chase girls or run from the heat?"

"Yeah, well, just don't you sweat it, LaTierri. I'm gonna make one of those teams, you'll see. In fact, you're gonna be there with me when it happens. I want you as my second."

"Ehh, Danny, I don't think you need a second to try out for a team. I mean, it's not like you need me to carry your body away."

"Well, Sonny-boy, you never know, you never know."

~ 15 ~

THE T-BIRDS WERE OUT IN FULL FORCE. ME, DANNY, Roger, Doody, and Kenickie were piled into Greased Lightnin' and whompin' over to the Palace to pick up the Ladies for the picnic in the park for Frenchy. The Ladies were waiting outside for us, and jumped into the car almost before we stopped. We wheeled down Moymensing Avenue and headed for Roosevelt Park.

We pulled into a sunny, deserted area of the park where some benches were, and laid out some blankets under the trees. Rizzo turned on her radio. Danny was pacing around. Doody sat on a trash can, and Kenickie passed out the suds. Me, Marsha and Frenchy were setting out the food, and Jan had already started eating.

Vince Fontaine was jivin' in the background on the radio.

Danny finally sat down on one of the picnic benches and drank his beer.

"Hey, Frenchy, when do ya start beauty school?" he asked.

"Next week. I can hardly wait. No more dumb books and stupid teachers."

Marsha let up a cigarette, then offered her pack around. "Anybody want a Vogue?"

"Yeah, Marsh. Ya got any pink ones left?"

"Eh, Marsh, I'll take one," I said. "And how about one for later?"

"Cheez, what a mooch!"

We started eating and drinking.

"Hey, Roge, you shouldn't be eatin' that cheeseburger. It's still Friday, y'know!" Doody yelled over from his post on top of the trash can.

"Son-of-a-bitch! Whatdja remind me for? Now I gotta go to confession." Roger took another bite of the cheeseburger.

"Doody, don't maul that magazine. There's a picture of Ricky Nelson in there I really wanna save," Frenchy said.

"I was just lookin' at Shelley Faberay's jugs."

Frenchy walked over to Doody and looked over his shoulder into the magazine.

"Ya know, Dood, lotsa people think I look just like Shelley Farberries."

"Ah, French, not a chance. You ain't got a set like hers."

"Yeah, well, I happen to know she wears falsies," Frenchy said.

"You oughtta know, Foam-Domes!" Doody said, and jumped off the trash can as Frenchy chased after him.

"Hey, right here!" Frenchy yelled, giving Doody the finger.

"Ya want another cheeseburger, Roger?" Jan asked.

"Nah, I think I'll have a Coke." Roger opened a soda for himself.

"You shouldn't drink so much Coke, Roge. It rots your teeth."

"No shit, Bucky Beaver," Roge said to Jan.

"Well, I ain't kiddin'. Somebody told me about this scientist once who knocked out one of his teeth and dropped it in this glass of Coke, and after a week, the tooth rotted away until there was nothing left."

"Yeah, Jan, that's really good. Christ! Whaddah ya think, I'm gonna carry around a mouthful of Coke for a week?"

Kenickie and Rizzo were under the trees wrapped up in each other, making out real heavy. Danny was playing around with Frenchy's boobs, while Frenchy was looking at him doing it, with kind of a funny look on her face. She wasn't flustered. She was curious.

"Hey, Danny, watch it, huh? Whaddah ya think you're doing, making a test?"

"They're real, Dood. You don't know what you're talking about."

So, we hung out eating and talking about falsies, and Rock and Roll singers, and Frenchy's going to beauty school, and we drank more beer and passed more time. Danny was trying to look cool, but I knew he was bugged about screwing up again with Sandy, and he was probably wishing that she was here. I was sitting with Marsha telling her about what had happened with Sandy on the field that day, and all Marsha said was, "What a jerk!"

We packed up for the day, and took a ride around the park in Greased Lightnin' before we headed back to the Palace.

~ 16 ~

I WAS IN THE MEN'S ROOM AT THE FROSTY PALACE,
propped up on the sink, leaning against the wall, with
my ears just about catching fire. Like a bloodhound-
detective, I scoped-in on the conversation coming
through the vent between the two bathrooms, which
was just above my head.

Ehey, like it makes me a little bit embarrassed to even
have to admit it, but I was eavesdropping on the Pink
Ladies—and that wasn't the embarrassing part. The Pink
Ladies were in the ladies' room, that was the worst of
this, but you can pick up on stuff in a bathroom conversation that you just can't get anywhere else. No lie.

Like I said, I felt a little weirded-out by this predica-
ment, but you got to understand that this was no
peeping-Tom or ear-to-the-glass-against-the-wall intru-
sion—this was first-class espionage. High ranked intel-
ligence work. Vital info coming in waves. I settled
down with a smoke, and tried to picture what was
happening on the other side of that wall as I recognized the Pink Ladies' voices . . .

"I don't get it," Rizzo said. "I mean, when Danny
Zuko can have a shooting star, why's he goin' after a
drip like Sandy? You tell me, 'cause I can't figure it."

"Riz, give Sandy a break, willya?" Marsha said. "Sure, she's a little different—"

"Different?!" Rizzo broke in. "C'mon. She's an out-an-out drip. A complete bust. I swear, sometimes she makes me feel like she's gonna give me penance or something."

"Well, maybe that's just what Danny likes about Sandy," Frenchy said. "You never can tell with a guy . . . Ehh, gimme a light . . . I mean, some guys go for girls that they can't get, just for that reason. It's a challenge to them, and that's all that counts for them."

"Did any of you guys ever stop to think that he might really dig her?" Marsha said. "You know, that ain't such an impossible thing, is it?"

"Marsh," Rizzo said, "Zuko ain't capable of diggin' anybody or anything 'less he's sure he'll get to the bottom of it first."

"Whew! You're a tough cookie, Riz. You don't give nobody credit for nothing. Danny ain't the snake you make him out to be, and you know it," Marsha said.

"You're right, Marsh," Frenchy said. "Danny has always been straight-from-the-shoulder with me."

"A'right, let me put it this way," Rizzo said. "What would you say about a guy who tells you he loves you, or even likes you a lot, but then he don't lay a hand on you . . . I'd say he's a creep!"

"Yeah?" Frenchy said, not really getting the point.

"Well," Rizzo continued, "if you was a guy and a girl wouldn't let you touch her, how'd you feel? A'right, so you don't let him go crazy on you and then post your name and number in phone booths across the country, but you gotta let the guy know you like him, or he ain't gonna stick around. It's that simple."

"Yeah, and that complicated, too. So, what're you saying, Riz?" Marsh asked.

"I'm saying that if Sandy wants Danny, she's got to

let him know that she would, if she could, but she can't, so she won't. Right now, she's a cold fish—and pretty soon she's gonna start to smell."

"Ahh, Riz," Frenchy said, "there're other ways of letting somebody you like know it. I mean, me and Doody manage it somehow."

"Doody's just a kid," Riz said, flatly.

"Yeah? And who the frig are you, Betty Crocker?" Frenchy yelled.

"Okay, sorry, Frenchy. I'm just on edge, that's all. I really didn't mean to come down on Doody," Rizzo said seriously. Frenchy nodded to her.

"A'right," Marsha said, "but it's still true what Frenchy said—there are other ways. Me and Sonny get pretty sexy, but we stay straight somehow. It's hard, sure. Guys think it's like a built-in thing for a girl to resist a guy, when it's just the other way around."

"Yeah, but the important thing is, no matter what, that you like the guy. And he likes you. After that, then you start to figure out what's going on. But you gotta have that feeling first," Frenchy said. "It's hard to say exactly what it is, except you get this feeling . . ."

"Yeah," Marsha said, "I think that's what Sandy and Danny got, this feeling—and they don't know what to do about it . . ."

"It's like something happens when you look into his eyes, and—"

Frenchy was cut off by Rizzo, who said, "Yeah, when I look into Kenickie's eyes, something really does happen. I get this feeling . . . yeah, this feeling deep down . . . and I don't know what it is, it's like . . . like I either have to puke or pee . . ."

The three girls all got a big laugh out of that, even though it was at Kenickie's expense.

I could just see the Ladies standing there in front of the mirrors, fixing their hair, painting up their eyes, and brushing their cheeks with pancake and rouge, while they thought they had the T-Birds wrapped up and cased, like puppy dogs in a show.

Frenchy was talking about what color she was going to dye her hair next, and Rizzo told her to try purple.

"You're just jealous, Rizzo," Frenchy told her. "Your hair won't even take dye. Maybe you should give it a paint-job."

Frenchy was laying it on Rizzo but good. Marsha from time to time was letting out a giggle.

"Ehey, what is this?" Rizzo said. "Why you guys jumping on my number today? Just 'cause I laid it out on Sandy, don't mean you got to get on me."

"So, you can give it out but you can't take it, huh?" Marsha said.

"It ain't that, Marsh. I can take it, all right, but it depends who's givin' and how."

"So, we suppose to reach some kind of verdict here today, or what?" Frenchy asked.

"What are you saying, French?" Rizzo asked.

"About Sandy. I mean, with the way you were talking about her, you made it sound like you didn't want her hanging out anymore."

"Ahh, it ain't that, French. First of all, who am I to say who hangs out and who don't? And, besides, she don't come around often enough to present problems, so to speak. So, I can't say that she really bothers me. It's just that I'm looking out for her own interests."

"Yeah? Since when, Riz?" Marsha asked.

"What's that mean?"

"Just was wondering if maybe you was interested in Danny again, that's all."

"Nah, that's old history."

"But history sometimes repeats itself," Frenchy said.

"You guys are full of it," Rizzo said lightly. "C'mon, let's take a spin in the Stude and see what's poppin'."

"A'right."

"Listen," Rizzo said, "Sandy's really okay, for what she is. She's just in the wrong crowd. What's she doing hanging out with us, and the T-Birds, and especially Danny Zuko. That's my point."

"Maybe she likes it," Marsha said. "Maybe she likes us, and the T-Birds, and Danny. And maybe we all like her. Didja ever think of that, Riz?"

"Ehey, what's with this 'like' shit? I never said I didn't like her, I just said she was a drip. If she ever wants to really make it, she's gonna have to turn in her prom dress—that's what I'm saying," Rizzo concluded.

"And, I'm saying, give her a chance, Riz," Frenchy said. "Maybe we can learn something from her, like she's trying to learn from us."

"Yeah, it's possible, but I don't know if I'm that hot on giving up everything I dig just 'cause it'll put me in good standing with Mamie Eisenhower. But, you're right, I'll be cool."

"Cool."

"To the Stude," Rizzo said.

When the Ladies split the bathroom, I sat on the other side of the wall thinking that we all had a lot to learn.

IT WAS PRETTY LATE SATURDAY NIGHT WHEN I GOT back to the corner. Me and Marsha had gone to the movies, but only to make out in the balcony, so I couldn't even tell you what was playing. I dropped her off at home, and then headed for the corner, knowing that somebody would be around. Danny was hanging out with Roger. Doody had already gone home. They were drinking some suds and lying low on the steps. I joined them and opened a beer.

We weren't saying much, except how we thought Danny would never make any of the school's teams.

"It's not only your attitude, Danny-boy," I told him, "it's your body."

"Yeah, and what'samatter with my body?" Danny flexed his arms, then ran his hands over his chest.

"Well, it's not that anything's wrong," Roger said, "it's just that nothin's really right about it. You know what I mean?"

"No, wise-ass, I don't," Danny said, taking a swig of beer.

"Danny, you got a good body, but you ain't an athlete, that's all," Roger explained. "What do you know about wheat germ, for instance? You ever lift weights?"

"Alright, you guys go ahead and talk. We'll see, that's all I got to say. We'll see."

"Ahh," Roger said, "is that the dulcet tones of that precision machine known as Greased Lightnin' that I hear cranking through the night?"

"Yeah, sounds like," I said.

Danny pointed down the street.

"Look at the cross-eyed headlights. Who else could it be?"

Greased Lightnin' came hobblin' up the street, lookin' in worse shape than she'd ever been in. Her grill was dented and her bumper was bent, and both fenders were creased and barely hanging on. Kenick rolled to a stop, and slowly got out of the car with his head hanging low. He was a vision of a bad luck story.

"Uhhh. Ohhhh. Christ." Kenickie was pained.

"You alright, man?" Danny asked, jumping up and taking him by the arm.

"Yeah, yeah, I'm fine, but look at my honey!"

Kenick slumped down on the steps.

"What the hell happened, Kenick?" I asked.

"We got trouble. We got big trouble!"

"Kenick, you gonna go on like this, or you gonna tell us what the hell happened?"

"Ahhh, you won't believe it. Me and Rizzo were parkin' down by the lakes, right. And it was really crowded tonight. Like, bumper to bumper. Somebody could'a sold tickets and made a fortune. Anyway, me and Rizzo finally found a spot, so we pull in and start making it.

"I should'a known from the beginning that nothing was gonna go right. First, we were neckin' pretty hot and heavy, so I figure she's ready, right. So she asks me if I got something, and I pull out my twenty-five-cent insurance policy, so Riz calls me a big spender. Anyway, I start to take it out and, I couldn't believe it, the damn thing was broken. I tried to tell Riz and all she could say was, 'how could it break?' So, I finally had to tell her that I bought it when I was in the seventh grade, right?"

"You dip, Kenick," Danny said.

"So, let me tell ya, will ya? All right, Riz is a little pissed at me, but we climb into the back seat anyway, and settle on making out. So, things were going pretty good, wrapped up in-tight here, a little bit of this and that there, and if I had windows they would'a been steamed up good, believe it . . ."

"Kenick," Roger said, "just tell us what happened to the car, will ya?"

"I'm gettin' to it. Relax. You wanna hear the story or you want the bare facts? Take it easy. I was saying, me and Riz was in the back seat rollin' around when all of a sudden, KA-BOOM! I came flipping over the back seat into the front and Rizzo is just about thrown outta the car. So, when I finally get around to my senses, I get outta the car and who the frig is there but Leo in his goddamn Hell's Chariot. The creep had backed up into my Greased Lightnin'. So, I says to him, 'Hey! What the hell you think you're doing?' And ol' Leo leans outta his window and says, like a real smart ass, 'Ya parked in a No Parking zone, pinhead.' So I told him, 'Whaddah ya, nuts? The whole place is a No Parking zone, ya creep!'

"Well, Leo gets outta his car, and only Riz is keepin' me from bustin' his head open, and Leo starts checkin' out Hell's Chariot, as if something might'a happened to it. The goddamn thing didn't have a scratch on it! But once I got a look at ol' Greased Lightnin', I could'a cried, honest! The baby was busted up right before my eyes. Well, ol' Riz is holding onto my arm at this point and I look into Leo's Hell's Chariot and see this Amazon chick sitting in the front, and she gives me this real sexy smile as she's takin' her bra off the rear-view mirror. So I turn on Leo and catch him makin' eyes at Riz, and, worse than that, Riz is digging it. Can you believe it? The whole goddamn night was a bust! Finally I tell Leo, 'I'm gonna make you pay for this, ya creep!' And ya know what he says to me? Get this—he says, 'I'll give ya seventy-five cents for the whole car . . . including your girl.' So, I busted loose from Riz, to cream his brains all over the friggin' car, but Leo jumped behind the wheel and laid rubber for a quarter-mile gettin' outta there."

"Wow." "Shit." "Damn." "He's a dead one."

"So, whaddah we do, Danny?" Roger asked.

"We gotta do something," I said.

"We wait," Danny said.

"Wait?" Kenick yelled. "Whaddah ya mean, wait?"

"We wait. Leo and the Scorpions are gonna make a move, and we'll be ready. Those guys are sneaky, and they ain't known for their fightin', so they'll probably do something sneakier. We just be ready for it."

Kenick got up and walked to his car.

"What about her?" Kenick asked, pointing to his car. "I gotta defend her honor, somehow. We gotta do something."

"It's a hopeless case, Kenick," Roger said.

Kenick killed him with his eyes.

"Junk it," I said.

"We won't have to do much to do that," Danny said. Then he added, "Nah, just kidding, Kenick. Look-it. I don't think it's so bad. In fact, it's okay. It's pretty good."

Kenick was brightening.

"No, I don't even think it's good . . . it's a major piece of machinery," Danny continued. "I said, a major piece of machinery! We can't eighty-six it."

"Yeah, tell 'em, Danny-boy!" Kenick yelled, patting the hood.

"We'll take it into Mrs. Murdock's Auto Shop at

school and have it ready to race in no time!" Danny was bringing Kenickie right out of his slump.

Danny walked around Greased Lightnin' as he continued to talk.

"Look at the lines. Look at the lights. Well, it needs a little work, but it's all here! It's hydramatic . . . systematic . . . automatic . . . aristocratic . . ."

"Yeah, yeah!" Kenick was egging Danny on.

"It's the best!" Danny yelled. "I tell you what it is . . . it's Greased Lightnin'."

"Yeah, Greased Lightnin'!" Kenick yelled.

Kenick and Danny slapped each other's hands.

"Greased Lightnin', you're our baby!" Danny said. "Dual exhaust! A good transmission! Fluid drive! Out, in and overdrive. We can do it! We can fix it! Greased Lightnin'— Go!!!"

For a second, we almost saw ol' Greased Lightnin' revved up and gleaming, shooting streams of hot exhaust, digging into the dust, wanting to cut loose. But as soon as we stepped back, all we could see was a big heap of red dented junk.

~ 18 ~

ON THE WAY OVER TO THE GYM FOR TRYOUTS, DANNY made me promise that I wouldn't say anything to anyone about what was about to happen, unless of course he made the team.

"Yeah, sure, Danny, only the good news'll get out," I assured him.

We popped into the gym and it seemed like most of the tryouts were over, and a lot of kids were just messing around on the equipment. Coach Calhoun was sitting in a chair, leaning against the wall, reading a magazine and dribbling a basketball.

Coach Calhoun was a guy in his 50s who at one time was probably an incredible athlete, but for some reason he never made it in the pros, so he was left with coaching as his livelihood. Along with this came the misfortune of having to coach at Rydell, where there really weren't enough athletes to go around. Although we managed to have some good teams, mostly it was the result of the same few athletes, like Finn, who played in all the sports. So, Coach Calhoun would usually find a spot somewhere on his team for anyone who wanted to play.

When Danny walked up dressed in his T-Birds' jacket, black T-shirt, black peg pants, and boots,

Coach Calhoun was definitely underwhelmed. He looked up from his magazine while continuing to dribble the basketball like it was an extension of his arm and checked Danny out from head to toe. Danny had a smoke dangling out of his mouth, and with one flick of his hand between dribbles of the ball, Coach Calhoun knocked the ciggie out of Danny's mouth.

"Ehey, that was pretty good," Danny said, impressed.

"A'right, kid, let's start with the first rule, cutting down to two packs a day."

The look on Danny's face didn't give Coach any encouragement on this point.

"What sports do you like?"

"Well, Coach, I'm kinda interested in cars."

"In athletics, son, you are the car."

Coach rose from his chair, still dribbling, and looked around the gym.

"How about the rings?" he asked Danny.

"Yeah. I installed a set of rings and valves a coupla weeks ago."

Coach rolled his eyes, then palmed the basketball and turned to Danny.

"Kid, what's your name?"

"Danny. Danny Zuko."

"Okay, Danny Danny Zuko, to begin with—you gotta change."

"Yeah, I know, Coach. That's what I'm trying to do, and that's why I'm here," Danny said sincerely.

"Your clothes, Zuko! Your clothes!"

Coach turned to me and said, "Who're you, his agent?"

I decided I should play the role, and simply nodded, put on my shades, and followed Danny downstairs to the locker room. Danny checked his leather, and in exchange was given trunks, jersey, jock, sneaks, and socks. He came out bouncing on his toes, looking like a green and white elf with greasy black hair.

When we came up, there was a pick-up game of basketball going on at the center court. It was a fast game being played with flash and finesse. Danny watched with great intensity.

Coach came over and wrapped his arm around Danny, for some reason taking a personal interest in Danny's newly found concern with sports. Probably Coach sensed something of a desperate case on his hands.

"Son, dribbling is an art. It's like yo-yoing without a string. Think you can do it?"

Danny studied the game for another moment, then gave the coach a single, abrupt nod of his head. Coach blew his whistle and the game stopped. The kids caught their breath.

"A'right, fellas, trying out a new man here. Hit it, Zuko. Take a breather, Schmidt."

The rest of the kids looked at Danny as if he was a new lamb being brought to slaughter. Danny shuffled self-consciously onto the floor. There was a moment of uncomfortable silence in which everyone was checking out Danny, but Danny threw hard looks all the way around the court and everyone knew where they stood. The kid with the ball winged it at Danny with some punch behind his throw. Danny caught the ball effortlessly, and stood motionless for a second, then gave the ball a few dribbles, getting used to the feel of it. Coach Calhoun sounded his whistle, and instantly Danny took off downcourt with the ball, getting faster and fancier with his dribbling as he approached the basket. Everyone on the court was playing against Danny. He didn't care, or know the difference. He never looked for anyone else to be on his side.

The kids on the court tried to block him, but Danny was dazzling, jukin' to one side, fakin' with his hips to the other, and finally making his break for the net.

He cut in under the hoop and went up for his shot, but was blocked in midair by a monstrously tall red-headed kid. The redhead couldn't hold onto the ball, and Danny swept it up before anyone else could get near it.

Coach Calhoun stood next to me on the sidelines smiling, and said, "Pretty good, huh? Not bad, huh?" I maintained my silence, but lifted my shades for a second just to let the light in.

Danny was circling the basket again, stalking the defensemen, waiting to make his move to the basket. He drew the forward out and curled around behind him, then broke in along the baseline. He came out under the net and hooked a shot up, and again it was blocked by the redhead, who came out of nowhere.

Danny again got the ball back, dribbled to the foul line, zeroed in on the redhead, and played him man-to-man. He drove right at him, faked a jump shot, and when the redhead tried to block the faked shot, Danny held out his foot and threw out an elbow, flipping the redhead to the floor. Danny then fired the ball cleanly through the hoop, as the redhead crumpled to the floor behind him.

Coach blew his whistle urgently. Danny turned to him smiling, pleased with himself, and said, "You don't have to stop the game on my account, Coach."

"Zuko, take a break!"

When Danny came over, Coach explained that there were certain rules in basketball that didn't allow for that kind of body contact. Danny looked at him and said, "But he kept blocking my shot." Coach said that the redhead was supposed to, that it was his job on the court. Danny simply said, "Well, if he can do it, and I can't, I don't wanna play."

"What else have you got?" I asked.

Coach led Danny over to the wrestling mats, where two wrestlers were sparring. One of them came off the mat, at Coach's signal, and gave Danny his head-guard and knee and elbow pads.

Danny was positioned on his knees beneath the other wrestler, who outweighed him by a good fifty pounds. At the sound of the whistle, Danny was clipped and flipped in a matter of seconds, and found himself under this big, fat kid who was sprawling on top of him with his armpits in Danny's face. The kid couldn't pin Danny, but Danny couldn't budge the fat kid either.

The fat kid was huffing and puffing, and managed to blurt out, "Give?"

Danny looked up at him and said, "Yeah."

As the fat kid rolled off, Danny wriggled free an arm and smashed the fat kid in the face. The kid looked at him for a second in disbelief, then collapsed to the mat.

Danny walked from the mat, throwing off his guard and pads, and said to the Coach, "Yeah, I know, they got rules. But I don't like to lose a fight just 'cause the other guy ties up my arms, ya know? I think I'd be better at something where nobody is screwin' around with my body."

"What about baseball?" I asked, lifting my shades.

Coach shrugged, then told Danny where he could get a uniform. He said he would meet him on the field behind the gym.

When we got to the field, a game was in progress. Coach Calhoun was on the bench taking notes on a clipboard.

"Zuko!"

Danny walked over to the bench, trying to get used to his baseball uniform.

"O.K., Zuk. I think you'll like baseball. The contact is not as close. Now, after this batter, I want you to pinch-hit." Coach slapped Danny on the back.

The batter hit a pop fly that was an easy out. Danny

walked up to the plate shouldering his bat, and dead-eyeing the pitcher.

Behind the plate the catcher was yelling, "Come, babe! Hum hard! Come, boy!"

Danny turned to him and said flatly, "I'm trying to concentrate." Which brought a laugh from the umpire, and silence from the catcher.

The pitcher wound up and fired a blazing pitch which Danny swung at and missed.

"Strike!" the ump yelled.

Danny narrowed his eyes at the ump and said, "Don't make such a big deal out of it. Everybody can see it was a strike."

The ump adjusted his mask and ignored Danny. The pitcher wound up and delivered a fat fast ball over the plate which Danny cracked far into left field, easily a stand-up double, at the least. Coach Calhoun was cheering. Danny took off for first. The umpire yelled, "Foul ball!"

Danny walked slowly back to the plate and looked at the ump with murder in his eyes. He reached out and grabbed the ump's facemask and pulled it away from his face, stretching the elastic band holding it on his head. "Wise guy, ehh?" Danny said, before letting go of the mask which snapped back onto the umpire's face.

Coach ran from the bench and led Danny off the field. He looked over his shoulder and saw the ump dusting himself and getting up off the ground somewhat dazed.

"Well, Zuk," Coach said pleasantly, "there are other things than contact sports."

For some reason, Coach was amused with Danny's antics, and almost seemed to encourage him.

"Like what kind of sports?" I asked.

Coach smiled, then said, "Track."

"You mean running?" Danny asked.

Summer romance

Rydell

High

Class

of

1959

Sandy

Danny

Rizzo

Kenickie

Sonny

Marty

The Thunderbirds and their dream car

Danny and Greased Lightning

Danny gives Sandy his school ring.

Sandy decides what to do.

Danny in love

**TOGETHER
FOREVER!**

"Ahh, Zuko, it's not just running . . . it's long-distance running. Something that requires stamina, endurance—"

"Me? A long-distance runner?" Danny cut him off in mid-sentence. Danny was amazed.

"Well, Zuk, there's not much else left for you to try. So you might as well give it a go, huh?"

"A long-distance runner . . ." Danny headed for the locker room to change again, this time to a track uniform.

I sat in the bleachers watching Danny circling the track, hyperventilating and probably near collapse, but in spite of it, he kept on running. There was something a little crazy in all of this, I thought. Madness in his method, so to speak. I mean, first of all, he was doing all this for Sandy. And all he really had to do was tell her how he felt about her, or, less than that, just be nice to her. But no, he had to be a jerk and let things get to this. Now, he was gonna be cramped up like crazy tomorrow morning, and still would be without Sandy, and probably still without having made any of the teams. Oh, he was a runner all right, but he'd never get a varsity letter for it. Lots of mean nasty letters, for sure, but not for his athletic performance.

As Danny was circling the far side of the field, Patty and the cheerleaders came onto the field in front of me, to practice their cheerleading. Following them was Sandy, talking with Tom, a big jock on Rydell's teams. Danny was rounding the bend when he caught sight of Tom and Sandy, chatting in front of the bleachers.

I watched Danny turn into the straightaway and knew that he was going to try to jump the hurdles that were set up right in front of where Tom and Sandy were talking. Why was it, I asked myself, that every time you get in a position where you're trying to impress a girl, you find yourself up against impossible odds? I rose from the bleachers and walked to the edge of the track, next to the hurdles.

Danny was striding into the hurdles sleek and smooth and fast, like running water. He took the first one with ease, then riveted his eyes on Sandy and Tom, but kept on running, clearing the next hurdle like a blind Olympian. But when he landed, he was greatly distracted by Tom, who had whispered something in Sandy's ear, to which Sandy broke into sexy little giggles. Danny flew into the next hurdle without ever leaving the ground. His legs twisted into each other, and he fell in a heap onto the broken hurdle.

Sandy suddenly rushed from Tom over to Danny, who was stretched out on his back with his arms spread. Sandy knelt beside Danny and took his head in her hand.

"Are you hurt? . . . Danny, talk to me! Are you all right?"

Danny struggled to prop himself on his elbows.

"Sure," he said uncertainly.

Danny had a glassy look in his eyes.

"Uhhh, where am I?"

"Danny, what's the matter?" Sandy grabbed his arm as he started to slip down.

"Hey, who are you?" Danny said, frightened by her touch.

"It's me, Sandy."

Sandy was confused as she watched Danny's face. He looked at her as if he had never seen her before. Sandy tried to laugh, then darkened with concern.

"Danny! Danny, snap out of it!"

"Do I know you?" he asked.

"Stop kidding me . . . Danny! Come on! Don't you remember anything?"

Sandy helped him to sit up. Danny looked around, trying to reassemble his surroundings.

"I seem . . . to remember . . . not being able . . . to get a date for the dance."

Danny smiled. Sandy laughed, delighted, then pushed Danny away.

"Sandy, come on. Who are you going with?"

She looked hesitatingly at Tom.

"So, you're going with him?" Danny said.

"Well, actually that depends."

"Yeah, on what?" Danny asked.

Sandy smiled at him. "On you, Zuko."

Danny pulled himself to his feet and joined hands with Sandy, and said, "He can stag it."

Danny looked over, past Tom, and called to me, "Sonny-boy! To the Palace!"

I ran after Danny and Sandy, and the three of us walked off the field and headed for the Palace, with Sandy in the middle holding onto both of us.

↞ 19 ↠

THE PALACE WAS PACKED AND SWINGING WHEN WE walked in. Bobby Darin's new hit, "Mack the Knife," was playing on the Northern Lights jukebox. Some couples were dancing, others were table hopping or standing in groups talking and jiving. Vi, one of the waitresses, was slinking through the crowd with a loaded tray.

"Ehey, Herbert, watch the sherbert!" Vi yelled, making her way to a table.

The Thunderbirds and Pink Ladies were scattered around the Palace. Once we moved into the crowd, Danny stiffened a little with Sandy on his arm taking possession of him. His face was going through changes, from a teen angel to a hotrod greaser, depending upon who he ran into, and whether or not Sandy was watching him.

"Ehey, Sandy, why don't we just go somewhere else?"

Sandy said only, "Dannn-ny," which was enough.

I saw Marsha by the juke and called her over.

"Yooh, Sonny, where ya been, lover-boy?" she said, giving me a big hug.

"Ehey, babe, handle with care, and don't mess the

hair. Give me a squeeze if ya please, but don't wrinkle the clothes or I'll bust up your nose."

"Sonny, suck wind, will ya, and gimme a hug!"

Boy, it was great to see Marsha. She was glad to see me too. We gave each other a big kiss. Then Marsha turned to Danny and Sandy and pecked each of them on the cheek.

Danny and Sandy jumped into a booth, while me and Marsha stood together talking next to them. The Palace was really jumping with action. Kenickie and Rizzo were in the corner making out, with Doody looking over Kenick's shoulder at Rizzo. He was making faces at her, but she had her eyes closed. Roger was hanging out with Marty at the counter. Finn was playing his sax to two beautiful girls by the jukebox. And Frenchy was standing alone by the door, with a scarf wrapped around her head, looking deflated in her beautician's uniform.

For a Monday, the Palace was really poppin'. I think it had something to do with kids revving up for the National Dance-off. It was a few weeks away but the girls were making themselves available. So the guys without dates could ask them.

It had not yet reached a point of desperation, so everybody without a date was still checking everybody else out, wondering who to make the move on, and when. Like, how high to shoot, and how low to scoop, when it got down to it. It had a lot to do with timing. I had it sewed up with Marsha, but I remembered last year, when I was trying to time it down to the wire. I wanted to ask Dotty, who was out of my league, but I kept putting off asking her while I tried to build up my nerve. In the meantime, not only had somebody who looked like a toad asked Dotty and she accepted, but by that time every other decent looking chick had also taken a date for the dance. I hesitated and lost big. My choices were limited to bookworms and weasels, and let's face it, nobody needs a date that bad. I went stag to the dance and brought along a pint of booze that Skippy sold to me. By the end of the night, I was good and drunk and never knew the difference.

But, like I said, there was still time before the pre-dance panic was on. You could see by the look in the eyes of those without dates that each of them was calculating the best chances, and keeping a daily check on the calendar. The guys could take three or four long shots, and still come up with a decent showing. The girls could shoot down eight or nine offers before having to make serious considerations. We all knew what was going on. We had all been involved in the pre-dance shuffling, and I for one was glad to be out of it this year. I squeezed Marsh a little tighter even at the thought.

Marsha and I were hanging onto each other when Ernie's son, Anthony, came running out from the kitchen. Anthony was seven years old, but could keep pace with any of the older guys, and sometimes leave them in the dust. He was a favorite of mine, and I think I was of his.

He ran up to me.

"Hey, hey, hey, Sonny-baby." Anthony giggled; he got a big kick out of imitating me.

"I know I hear somebody, but I just can't see 'em. Who's calling me?" I said, looking around and over Anthony's head.

"Me."

"Who?"

"Me."

"Who's me?"

"Anthony!"

"Anthony. I remember the name, but I can't place the face." I still hadn't looked down. He was pulling at my leather.

"Anthony? Anthony? Cheez, it really sounds familiar," I said, scratching my head.

"DiFebbo. Anthony DiFebbo. Remember that name, kid, 'cause it'll cost you next time ya forget." Anthony was doing a pretty good imitation of me. I bent over and scooped him up, setting him on the table where Danny and Sandy were sitting. Danny had barricaded himself and Sandy behind several menus propped across the center of the table like a wall. Behind the menus, Danny and Sandy kissed and held hands.

Anthony was duded up in his little greaser's outfit today. He looked more like a midget than a kid.

"Ehey, Danny," Anthony said, still imitating me, "what are ya doin' behind the scenes, ehh?"

"Yooh, Ant," Danny said, peeking up over the menus, "get lost, willya?"

"Sure, ya think it's easy, just 'cause I'm small, right? Didja ever try to get lost in a pink and white room? Try it sometime. My mother finds me no matter what."

"Ant, let's quit playing around. What do I gotta do to get rid of you?"

"Now you're talking, Danny-boy. Take me to the movies, and we'll call it even," Anthony said, standing on the table and looking over the menus at Danny and Sandy.

"A'right, kid, ya got it. Now, beat it."

"See ya, Danny. I dig your chick."

Sandy smiled at Anthony. He shrugged, and flipped up the collar on his leather, then took a running start before jumping off the table into my arms. He gave me a quick little hug, then pushed himself off, jumped to the floor and ran back to the kitchen.

"A'right, guys, let's break it up here," Marsha said, sliding into the booth next to Sandy. I sat down next to Danny.

"He's a crazy little kid," Danny said about Anthony. "You know he's not gonna let me forget about

113

the movies, don't you. Last time I promised him something, some comics I think it was, he was calling me up at home to remind me."

Vi, the waitress, came over to our table.

"Hiya, guys and gals, what'll it be?"

"I just want a cherry soda. What do you want, Danny?" Sandy said.

Danny leaned back and thought a moment, then said loudly, "I don't think I'm very hungry. A double Polar Burger with everything . . . and a cherry soda with chocolate ice cream."

"That sounds good," Sandy changed her mind. "Make it two."

"Sonny? Marsh?" Vi asked.

"Uhh, Marsh," I said, going over my desperate and embarrassing financial situation, "I got twenty-three cents. Let's chip in for a Dog-Sled Delite."

"I swear," Marsh said, "I don't know where the money goes. A dime here. Fifteen cents there. Hell, before you know it, you burned half a buck without seeing it go up in smoke. Yeah, Sonny, let's split the Dog."

Vi nodded, just as Kenickie and Rizzo blew over to our table. They squeezed into the booth. Vi watched us pack ourselves together.

"Okay, Kenick and Riz. What'll it be, a shoehorn?"

"Riz, you got a couple of quarters? We could split an Eskimo Pie," Kenick said.

"Ehey, Kenick, make ice! My Dutch-treat days are over," Riz said.

"You must plan on staying home a lot," Kenick shot at her.

Rizzo narrowed her eyes with a look that could've killed.

"Vi, just bring the Dog-Sled Delite with four spoons," I said.

"And a knife," Kenick said, baring his teeth at Rizzo.

Vi walked away shaking her head.

"So, how's it going, Zuko?" Kenick said. "Long time no see."

"It's cool, Kenick. It's swinging, you know . . ." Danny laid out his rap. Sandy shot him a dirty look, which settled him down.

"Yeah, well, looks like Danny's back . . . and Sandy's scratching it," Rizzo said, cracking her gum.

"And how's the famous Sonny LaTierri and his swinging momma Marsha?" Kenick said, jiving.

"Tight as a drum," I said.

"And a lot more fun," Marsh added.

Doody and Frenchy pulled up another table and some chairs.

"Greetings, pals and gals," Doody said.

"Yeah, hi," French said, without much enthusiasm.

"Hey, Frenchy, this is on me," Doody said. "Get yourself some toothpicks or a glass of water. In another couple of months you'll be taking us out—a working girl with income."

Frenchy adjusted the scarf on her head, and seemed a bit removed from everyone else.

"Well, they don't pay you too much to start with. But get what you want, Dood, I can cover it."

"Thanks, French. I don't get my allowance 'til Friday."

"You still get an allowance, Dood?" Kenick asked.

"When I'm a good boy, yeah."

"Cheez, your father wanna adopt another son?"

A waitress passed by the table with a tray loaded with food. When she turned her back, Kenick snatched a burger off the tray as it went by and ate half of it in one bite. Rizzo reached across the table and grabbed what was left of the burger from Kenick. He had food stuffed in and out of his mouth. He made a weird face at Rizzo and stuck out his tongue.

"Uggh! You pig!" she yelled.

"Oh, baby!" Kenick sighed. "I love it when you talk dirty." He polished off what was left of his burger.

Vi arrived with our food and drinks, and we ripped through it all, like instantly.

Under the table, I could feel Danny and Sandy playing footsies. I looked at them and they were holding hands and gazing into each other's eyes. Sandy finally broke the spell.

"Danny, I want to invite you over to meet my folks. Can you come Sunday?"

"Nah, I don't like parents," Danny said, for our benefit. "And, I hate Sundays," he added with emphasis.

Well, I have to admit, Sandy was definitely being a little corny and old-fashioned, but, on the other hand, Danny was being an absolute shit, and was being stupid on top of it. I mean, unless you're talking to a goat or somebody with the sensitivity of a telephone pole, you just can't say shit like that and expect to get away with it.

Sandy turned a kind of greenish-purple, and tightened her face and snarled, "Danny Zuko, apologize or I'm leaving!"

Danny looked at her like she was nuts. I don't know what could have been on his mind, but it couldn't have been much.

Sandy stood up, which wasn't the easiest thing to do in a booth, and crawled over Marsha and Kenickie, then stood in the aisle at the end of the table.

"Well?" Sandy put her hands on her hips, looking mean and defiant, but under that she looked hurt.

"Danny-boy," I said between my teeth and under my breath, "if you got an ounce of brain in all that jive, get the frig up and out, man. Now."

"Sandy, look, let's take a walk and talk this over, huh?"

As we were getting up to let Danny out of the booth, Sandy ran out of the Palace ahead of him.

He was going to have to do a lot of talking and dancing in his shoes to sweeten Sandy's mood. She had been passing up too many chances to hand Danny his head, or clip his wings, and this looked like he had pushed her one time too many.

"Good luck, lover-boy," Kenickie called after Danny as he walked out after Sandy.

"Kenick, just shut up, will ya? You give yourself a bad name every time you open your mouth," Rizzo said.

"Hey, Riz, what is it with you today? You got the personality of a wet mop."

"Kenick, look, don't start with me."

"Yeah, well, maybe I'll finish with you."

Rizzo rose from the booth.

"Finish this, jerk!" Rizzo picked up Doody's milkshake and turned it upside down on Kenick's head. The strawberry shake dripped down all over Kenick's face, and some splashed over onto Frenchy. Kenickie was stunned and speechless.

"To you from me, Pinky Lee," Rizzo said, then turned to Frenchy and said, "Sorry about that." Rizzo stomped out of the Palace.

"RIZZO!" Kenick screamed and chased after her, wiping the shake from his hair and face.

We all helped Frenchy clean herself up. Vi brought over napkins and rags. Marsha was wiping Frenchy's face for her, when Frenchy took off her scarf since the milkshake had slipped underneath. We took one look at Frenchy's hair and, in one voice, gasped. It was striped. Blue, orange, white, and green stripes. Frenchy was so busy cleaning off the milkshake, she didn't realize that her hair was exposed until she looked up at our faces.

"Oh, I ran into a little trouble in tinting class," she said timidly.

"Looks like an Easter egg," Doody whispered to me.

"In fact," Frenchy continued, "I ran into trouble in all my classes. Beauty school sure isn't what I thought it would be."

"Nothing ever is," Marsha said.

"Well, I dropped out . . ."

"Ahh, Frenchy," Marsha said, "what'll you do?"

⟵ 20 ⟶

. . . "Well, let me tell you about this cra-zy dream I had, which happened the night after I decided to drop out of beauty school. The weird thing is, I'm not completely sure that I was dreaming. I remember just kind of drifting off in a daze, but not really falling asleep . . .

"Anyway, there I was in bed, trying to figure out what to do with my life, when all of a sudden I heard this spooky angelic guitar being played outside my window. I got up out of bed and there outside my window was this gorgeous guy, dressed in white, with big beautiful white wings. God! He was really the most!"

"Oh, yuck!" Doody said. "Just give us the dream, willya French, and forget the romance, huh?"

"What're ya jealous, Dood?" Frenchy asked.

"Yeah, sure, over a dream."

"Okay," Frenchy continued, "so this absolute hunk of a guy, who called himself Teen Angel, was flying outside my window with guitar music coming from somewhere in the background. Suddenly, Teen Angel jumped, or actually flew, through my window, and before he landed on my bedroom floor everything turned

119

white! Like, all of a sudden I was in heaven! There were clouds and a bright white staircase that disappeared into the sky.

"So, Teen Angel flew down and landed in front of me. Coming down the staircase behind Teen Angel was a band of Angelettes. The crazy thing was that these Angelettes looked like they had been run out of a beauty shop in the middle of their appointment. They had their hair up in torpedo rollers and were dressed in smocks. Some of them held out their hands and waved them, drying off their nails. It was absolutely crazy. And when I looked closer, their faces resembled the Pink Ladies.

"So, there I was with Teen Angel, who looked a lot like Frankie Avalon with dark wavy hair and a terrific sexy smile and soft kiss-me lips, and—"

"Ehey! Enough already, huh? We get the idea!" Doody said.

"Okay, okay," Frenchy conceded. "I was just fillin' in the details. So, I was saying, Teen Angel looked really good, dressed in his white sweater with the collar up, white chinos, white boots, and he had an enormous white comb sticking out of his pocket. He took one look at me and then held my face between his hands and called me 'Venus.' "

"Yeah, sure, French," I said. "Tell me another one."

"Sonny, shut up, and don't disturb other people's dream, willya?" Marsha yelled.

She was right. I shut up.

"Yeah, let me tellya," French said, undeterred. "Teen Angel takes me and leads me through these clouds, and it's like me and him and heaven—oh yeah, and the weirded-out Angelettes on the staircase—but to me it was only me and Teen Angel. I was working myself up for the ultimate, you know, 'cause I figured Teen Angel didn't make the trip for anything less. I knew all along that this was the way it was supposed to happen when it happens. Anyway, it beat the hell out of the back seat of any Chevy. So, Teen Angel walked with me through the clouds, then he turned to face me. I know that this is it, I'm sure of it, so I closed my eyes and puckered up and you know what that creep did? He started lecturing me. I couldn't believe it! I mean all of a sudden things went from best to worst.

"Not only did Teen Angel say that my story was a sad one to tell, he said I was the most screwed-up kid on the block! Oh, geez you guys, what am I going to do? I know he was right when he said that my career is washed up. On top of that he reminded me I couldn't even get a trade-in on my Beauty School smock!

"Teen Angel really rubbed it in. I mean he said 'Beauty School dropout, Beauty School dropout!' over and over again. He knew I flunked my midterms and that I even failed shampoo!

"Well he went on like this and pretty soon I started to get pissed but I didn't have nowhere else to go and I didn't know how to get out of the dream. So, I was stuck . . . listening to this stuff.

"By this time he was really giving me a speech. He said at least I could have fixed my wardrobe up after spending all that dough to have the doctor fix my nose up. Teen Angel said to move it! That dreams don't mean a thing unless you got the drive and Teen Angel said, 'Honey, you ain't got the drive.'

"So finally I said to him, 'Look, Teen Angel, what do you want me to do, since you seem to know everything?'

"He replied that if I had a diploma I could really be cool. . . . That I should forget the combs and curlers and go back to high school. It was really a warning and strong advice I could tell cuz then he kind of threw his arms up in the air and looked up to the sky and said if I didn't listen to him . . . if I couldn't promise to try he might just as well go back to his malt shop in the sky.

"Then he took off, and the Angelettes and heaven with him, just like that!" Frenchy huffed.

"That's a pretty crazy dream," Marsha said.

"Yeah, but you know what the strangest part was . . . as soon as Teen Angel left, I was back in bed, laying there the same way I was when he came. I mean, I never really woke up, 'cause I didn't think I was ever really asleep."

"C'mon, French, what're you trying to lay on us?" Dood asked.

"You saying you think Teen Angel really paid you a visit?" I asked.

"All I'm saying is, I'm not completely sure it was a dream, that's all. And, oh, this is the most important part—I decided to go back to Rydell."

"Great!"

"Well, next time you see Teen Angel, give him my phone number, willya French?" Marsha said.

We all laughed, including Frenchy.

"Yeah, sure Marsh," she said. "You'll be the first."

⌐ 21 ⌐

WHEN I SAW DANNY THAT NIGHT, I TOLD HIM ABOUT
Frenchy's Teen Angel, then asked him what had happened when he split the Palace chasing Sandy. He had
a hard time talking about it, but I could tell it was on
his mind and buggin' him, so he laid it on me.

. . . After Danny left the Palace, he chased Sandy
and finally caught up with her, and held her by the
arm.

"Sandy, where're ya goin'?"

Sandy shook his hand off of her arm and turned
her back to him.

"Where I go is no longer any of your business!"
she said, and crossed the street.

Danny ran ahead of her, then turned to face Sandy,
as he peddled backwards in front of her.

"So, what's the big deal? I'm sorry, okay. Really,
Sandy. But I don't know why you got to get mad at
me just 'cause I don't like parents or Sundays . . ."

"It's not that. It's your attitude. The way you say
things. You're a punk, Danny, and you're inconsiderate, besides. What? Do you get some cheap thrill when
you put me down in front of your friends? Well, let
me tell you something, Danny Zuko, if you had any
sense you'd know that your friends think you're a real

jerk when you act like that. You're *not* cool, Danny, you're just dumb!"

Sandy tried to walk around him, but Danny feinted from side to side, blocking her way.

"So, what do you want me to do? I already said I was sorry. You wanna make a public display? Hang a sign on me. 'Danny Zuko—dumb jerk and very uncool.' Should I lie down in the street or something?"

Sandy decided that since she couldn't walk around him, she would try to walk through him. She balled her arms together, and tucked her head down and walked straight at Danny.

Danny continued his plea, walking backwards as he yielded to Sandy's advances, and just as he said, "Well, least I'm not a creep," he went down, falling backwards, tripping over the curb.

Sandy cracked up. Danny looked up at her from the sidewalk and broke into a smile. She offered him a hand and helped him to his feet.

"Uhh, thanks, Sandy," Danny said. "Ha, I really do feel like a jerk."

"Well, that's only because you are, but there are worse things that you could be."

They walked to Girard Park and headed for a bench.

"Sandy," Danny said when they sat, "I don't wanna keep getting you mad at me, 'cause I don't really want to and I don't mean to. Uhh, I want you to know that, ehhh," Danny looked around then said, almost to himself, while running the words together, "I-really-like-you-a-lot-Sandy."

"Mean it?" she asked softly.

Danny finally turned to face Sandy as he slid closer to her on the bench.

"Sandy, I don't really know how to talk about these things, so I might sound like a sap, but I think you're . . . terrific, and wonderful, and . . . pretty. You're the nicest girl I ever met."

Danny slipped his hand around Sandy's.

"Danny, I'm sorry I got mad at you, and said all those things, because . . ." Sandy looked down at her hand in Danny's, "I really think you're pretty special yourself."

Danny perked up. "Ehey, like me and you, we're the best! Huh? Nah, better 'n that. Me and you, Sandy, we're the best of the best!"

"Yeah?" Sandy was giddy. "You really think so?"

"Baby, just look at us!"

Sandy squeezed his hand.

"Danny, you still want to take me to the dance?"

"Yooh, after all this, who else, huh? You're the one, baby. You start my heart, and put thump in my pump."

"And, you, Danny, uhh, you put, uhh, zing in my ring, and heat in my sleep." Sandy giggled loosely.

She told Danny she had to be getting home. When they got to the corner of her street, Sandy said, "You can leave me here, Danny. I don't think you're dying to meet my parents, huh?"

"Not today, Sandy. Not today. But some time. Just let me work up to it. I mean, I have a hard enough time with my own parents, let alone trying to break ice with yours."

"I understand. No big deal." Sandy smiled.

"But some time . . . and soon," Danny assured her.

When Danny told me he said that to Sandy, I wondered if those were famous last words—"Some time and soon." Danny said that he left Sandy at the corner of her street, but stayed around long enough to make sure that she got safely into her house. He was extremely proud of this noble gesture, but considering that it was the middle of the day, and Sandy lived only three houses in from the corner, I thought he was making a little more out of it than there really was.

It was good to see Danny finally trying to come around and face the fact that he could, conceivably, like this girl, maybe love her, if he would let himself. That was the problem. Sandy obviously liked Danny. But somehow Danny thought that to keep someone liking you you had to mistreat them. He had a long way to go, but Sandy could get him there.

⌐ 22 ⌐

WE BROUGHT GREASED LIGHTNIN' INTO AUTO SHOP
at school after Leo the Scorpion banged it up, and we
worked on it regularly. It was coming along slowly,
but looking better all the time. Mrs. Murdock was a
terrific help on it. She really got involved in fixing up
Greased Lightnin', especially when we told her we
were planning to race at Thunder Road.

The biggest problem was getting parts for the car.
If we were in the middle of doing some work and
realized we needed a part that wasn't available in
shop, we'd have to stop working because we couldn't
get our hands on anything until after nightfall. If it
was something easy, like a taillight, one of us would
run out to the school's parking lot and lift it off a
teacher's car. But when we got down to carburetors
and pistons, we needed the cover of night to promote
the necessary parts.

That night on the corner, we ran over Kenickie's
checklist for Greased Lightnin'. She wouldn't be out
of the shop in time for the dance, but if everything
went according to schedule Mrs. Murdock said
Greased Lightnin' would be ready to race before
school ended. Kenick ran down his checklist.

"Well, I'm happy to report that we no longer need

127

a hand brake, spare tire, or battery. But what we do need is a tail pipe, windshield, and . . . what? Roge, what's this word?"

"Solenoid. It helps start the engine."

"Yeah, got to have one," Kenick agreed.

"Hard to steal," Danny said. "Need to take the whole ignition assembly."

"Yeah, so since when has that stopped us?" Doody said.

Kenickie beamed.

"A'right, let me run over this again. Tail pipe, windshield, solidnoid—actually, let's change that to ignition assembly, complete—and for now, let's throw in a fan blade. That should keep us busy tonight, and tomorrow in shop."

"Check," Danny said, taking the list from Kenick. "Okay, Doody, you get the tail pipe, that's quick and easy. Roge, you and Kenick get on the ignition. You can break it down quicker than any of us. Oh, Dood, while you're at it, pick up a fan blade; you'll need an adjustable wrench for both jobs. And me and Sonny'll get the windshield. No sweat."

"Sure," I said, with little confidence.

Danny pointed to each of the T-Birds. "Doody, you go with Roger and Kenick and head south. Me and Sonny'll go east. Be careful. Be smart. And be quick. See you back here."

We set out for the booty hoping to nail down a quick hit. Danny and I each had our jackknives, which was all Danny said we'd need for the job.

I realized we could be out for the rest of our lives looking for a windshield to fit Greased Lightnin'.

"Naw, naw," Danny said. "Roger told me that any Chevy from '48 to '53 will fit Greased Lightnin', as long as it's a convertible model."

"I don't really see why he needs a windshield so bad. He don't even have a roof for that thing."

"Yeah, well, Sonny-boy, we'd better mark the car we hit tonight, because we'll probably be back tomorrow night for the top."

"Some lucky owner will be thrilled."

We walked down the dark side of the street, casing the cars parked on both sides of the street. Some people had garages in the back of their houses, and we thought it might be worth checking out. It would be the safest place to work, if we found an open garage door and the right car. It was a very long shot, about 30-1 I'd guess, if I was laying odds.

As it turned out, I wished I could have laid a bet. On our first block behind the houses, we found a garage opened with a '51 Chevy convertible parked inside. The top was even down, which would make it a snap to cop the windshield. We worked by the light of the moon and had the stripping removed in a few minutes, and had the glass popped out a while later. The whole job took about five minutes. We were back on the corner inside of twenty minutes after we set out. A very lucky night.

We placed the windshield over the windshield of another car parked on the corner, in case the cops came by, which they did from time to time, just to check us out. They'd never see it there.

The gods must have been with us that night, 'cause we made out like bandits. Half an hour later, Doody, Kenick, and Roger came back, loaded down with parts. We snuck into Roger's basement, stashed our take for the night, and went back to the corner to kill the rest of the night. In the morning we would all stop by Roger's and take something with us to auto shop.

~ 23 ~

THE COLD WEATHER HAD US HIBERNATING, SEEING
each other mostly at school during lunch, and maybe
one night together on the weekends, when we would
go to a movie, or hang at the Palace. Otherwise, we
sat around in each other's basements, playing pi-
nochle, watching television, or shooting the breeze.

In the midst of this winter freeze, tragedy struck
our lives. It came to us over the radio on a newsflash
bulletin. Vinnie Fontaine interrupted a song. We knew
then it was very bad news.

Danny, Kenick, me and Roger were all in my basement, hanging around, listening to Vinnie's program,
and working up a design for Greased Lightnin's
paint job.

I remember "Teenager in Love" by Dion and the
Belmonts was on the radio at the time, and was a very
hot song. Then in the middle of it, Vinnie stopped
the music.

"This is a W-A-X-X News Bulletin . . . just in! . . . A
plane which was transporting Ritchie Valens, Big Bopper, and Buddy Holly, after their concert, has crashed
in Iowa. All three of the singers are dead. . . ."

Vince continued with details of the crash, and the
concert tour they had been on, but we were all too

stunned to listen. We had grown up with these guys, had shared some of our best times with them, and now they were dead just like that, and none of them was really that much older than we were. We felt as if we had known them personally. They were friends in a very real way, and would always be missed like friends.

Vince didn't really say much once he finished the bulletin. Unless he was percolating at a mile a minute, he wasn't really much good with words. He played "Peggy Sue" and "That'll Be the Day." Between songs he said, "You know, Buddy was only 22." Then he played "Chantilly Lace" by the Big Bopper, and ended with "Ooh, My Head," by Ritchie Valens. It was a sad and fitting tribute.

We spent the rest of the day talking softly about the singers, mostly going over what it meant to have someone we cared about suddenly die.

"First it was James Dean a few years ago, and now this," I said.

"Shit, what a way to go—a plane crash," Kenick said, almost to himself.

"Yeah," Roger said, "and what a way to wind up—face down in the snow."

"Somewhere in Iowa," I added.

"You guys know what?" Danny said quietly. "It's only the beginning . . . for us, I mean. I don't think from here on out that we're going to be having too many more new idols—we're just gettin' too old for that stuff. But what's gonna happen is—all of our old idols, the people we grew up lookin' up to, they're all gonna fade on us, or die. . . . It's lousy, and I don't like it."

There was something too true and final in Danny's words. In his own way, he sometimes had a real sad understanding of things.

We talked of things to look forward to. There were

three of them—women, the coming-out of Greased Lightnin', and warm weather.

We decided to take a walk over to the Palace, and see how everybody else was holding up under the news. When we walked in, the Pink Ladies were all seated in one booth. Everybody else was at a table, or sitting at the counter. There was hardly any movement in the whole place. The jukebox was playing. It was Buddy Holly singing "Maybe Baby."

The four of us stood in the doorway of the Palace listening to the song, and when it was over we nodded to each other and realized that there was really nothing to talk about. At least not today.

I told Danny I thought it was a good night to follow up on his promise to take Anthony to the movies. We walked into the kitchen and found him in the back doing his homework. We cleared it with Ernie, then told Little Anthony (we nicked him after the singer) that we were going to the flicks tonight.

We thought he would be overwhelmed. Instead, he looked up from his notebook, and shrugged his shoulders.

"Naw, I don't think so," he said. "I mean, thanks anyway. I just don't feel like it."

"Okay, Ant. See ya later."

"Yeah," he said, and lowered his head into his homework again.

I guess nobody felt like doing anything that day. Not even Little Anthony, who didn't even know who Buddy Holly was, but seemed to feel bad about him just the same.

AT THE HOP

～ 24 ～

IT HAD FINALLY GOTTEN DOWN TO IT. THE NATIONAL
Bandstand Dance-Off was coming up Friday night on
live TV from Rydell's gym. All week in school, things
were a little crazy. Everybody had the jitters. Kids
were dancing in the halls, practicing and getting
pointers. Classes were noisy and full of action. We all
had a really hard time staying still.

Even kids like Wayne, who normally weren't nuts,
were getting stir crazy. Wayne had plans for college,
med school, and marriage; his home, his car, and his
kids. In short, Wayne had a line on the rest of his life
and he was reeling it in. He was as steady a rollin'
man as any of us ever seen. But today he went crazy
in the hall, right there in front of Principal McGee
and everyone. He ran down the hallway beating the
lockers with a stick, then took down a fire extinguisher
and sprayed the wall, and generally was insane. He
had to be subdued by Coach Calhoun.

Me and Danny were sitting in study hall by the
windows, where we could talk about the chicks in the
classroom and check out the action outside the
windows.

Pearly Pease, who also taught Chemistry, was our
study hall monitor. Pearly Pease was basically a jerk,

and it looked like his wife, or his mother, or both of them, beat him up daily and with pleasure. Pearly was getting to be an old man, but he still looked like a kid, and was a very nervous guy. When he was upset, he'd shake all over and stutter. He was a very sad man, but what was worse, we made merciless fun of him whenever we had a chance.

So Pearly Pease was sitting at the desk in the front of study hall reading a book, while the rest of the class busied themselves, with playthings mostly. Comics, makeup kits, tops, you know the stuff you study in study hall.

"Too damn quiet," Danny said, "it's driving me nuts. I swear, if I don't do something quick, I think I'm gonna scream. I'm getting the nerves bad, Sonny."

Danny didn't do anything quick, but he did scream. Loudly and fiercely, he cut loose with a terrific ear-piercing yell. He cried, "The ants! The ants! I got the ants, bad!"

I howled with laughter. Danny decided it was time we did a number together.

"So, Mr. Sonny LaTierri, Mr. Big-Shit-Shot, Mr. Eyetalian-Tight-Ass, Mr. Romance-in-the-Streets—you think it's funny? A man loses his mind right in front of you and you laugh?"

Danny was great. He was on his feet shaking. Pearly had jumped out of his chair, and without meaning to, he was imitating Danny, on his feet shaking. The rest of the class didn't know what the hell was happening.

"Shove it, Zuko!" I said, giving him the finger.

In one swift motion, Danny ran from the window, flung it open, and grabbed me by the collar and dragged me to the open window. Pearly Pease shrieked.

"Apologize, Sonny," Danny threatened.

"Like I said, Zuko, SHOVE IT!"

Danny wrapped his other hand around my waist and flipped me over his shoulder and out the window.

"Ohhhhhhh, mmmmmmmmmmmmmmmmy Ggggg-ggggod!" Pearly screamed.

Outside the window was a metal guardrail that ran along the ledge below the glass. I had a firm grip on the rail, and hung quietly below the window, listening to the action overhead.

Danny was blocking the window from everyone, as he yelled, "Don't nobody get any closer, or I swear I'll jump next!"

Pearly sounded a mess. Danny chuckled.

"Don't sweat it, Pearly. I never felt better in my life. I just needed to kick out the jambs, you know what I mean? Ahh, I feel so much better now though. . . ."

Pearly must have come closer. Danny yelled, "Get away from me! Don't you come any closer, or *you* go next! And there's no sense standing around watching me 'cause you only make me nervous, and that's not good considering the mood I'm in, you know what I mean? I NEED TO RELAX!" Danny screamed. He turned his back to Pearly and looked out the window, down toward the ground. He winked at me when we caught each other's eye.

"Ugggh. Don't even look. What a mess," Danny said, turning back to Pearly. "Pearly, leave me alone, will ya? And go get somebody to clean up that slop down there. God, Italians are really ugly spread across the sidewalk like that. . . ."

I heard Pearly gag and run out of the classroom. Danny reached over and pulled me into the room. Everyone in class went from shock to laughter and smiles. They had a feeling something was up, but they weren't quite sure what it was.

I dusted myself off, and slapped hands with Danny,

who was beaming at his own performance. We took our seats and went back to reading our comics.

Pearly Pease burst back into the room, dragging the security guard and Principal McGee behind him. He rushed right past me and Danny and ran to the window, hitting his face against it before he realized it was closed. He slid open the window in a panic, knowing that things had probably gotten worse by this time, and stood back and pointed down at the ground, before he himself had looked out.

The guard and McGee walked hesitantly to the window, and slowly leaned out and looked down. McGee whispered something to the guard, who nodded with understanding to her and left the room. McGee put her arm around Pearly and led him to the window, gingerly, and said in a motherly tone, "See, it's okay. Really, it's all okay. It's over. Somebody must have cleaned him up and taken him home."

The kids in class were great. No one said a word or even looked up. Pearly suddenly jumped back from the window and looked over to see me and Danny sitting in our regular seats, reading our regular comics, and not paying him any mind, as usual.

He started to gag on his own words and jump up and down as he tried to speak. He flayed his arms at me and Danny, and held McGee by the wrist.

"Bbbbbbbbbbbut, th-th-th-th-those bbbbbbboys, th-th-th-they . . ." He went on at great length, but with little results. McGee finally tired of pacifying him, and told him, "All right, Mr. Pease, I think I understand the situation quite perfectly. Now, you go have some coffee and I'll finish your study hall for you."

Pearly walked out unsteadily, and McGee came up to me and Danny.

"Now, you two, I don't even want to hear your side of it, because I didn't get his side. But I understand enough about these things to know something happened here, and even though I don't know what it was, I know LaTierri was responsible."

"Ahh, yooh, that ain't fair," I said.

McGee pulled out her pad of detention slips and started writing.

"Sonny, I'm giving you three days' detention, for what I *don't* know about what you did—call it general principles. Danny, just take a warning, and a lesson from your friend here."

The bell rang, saving me from a lecture. Hell, it was more than three days' detention worth of fun. I got off easy. It was one of those days, in one of those weeks.

— 25 —

IT WASN'T ONLY IN SCHOOL THAT THINGS WERE CRAZY that week. Every night the Palace was packed with panicky guys and girls looking for a last minute hook-up for the dance. Marsha and me had made our arrangements to go with Danny and Sandy. My cousin Finn was lending me his car for the occasion, since he was having one of his girlfriends drive him. So just about everything was set.

On Tuesday, my old man laid some bucks on me for a shirt and new shoes. My mother told him she didn't want to be disgraced on national television because her son looked like a pauper. I probably could have put the press on for a new suit, saying that my old suit made me look like a needy little immigrant, but if they sprang for a new suit, they might expect me to wear it after the dance. So I sent my black suit to the cleaners and settled for a shirt and shoes.

We had a special meeting on the corner on Wednesday night to get our signals straight for the dance.

"A'right," Danny said, "if any of us wins the contest, when you go to get the prize, hold the camera until the rest of us got a chance to get to the stage. Then introduce us as your friends. Got it?"

"Who you goin' with?" Doody asked Kenickie.

"Are you and Rizzo still broken up?" Roger asked.

"I lost track," Kenick said. "But I'm not going with her. I'm gonna have the hottest date there, you'll see." He wouldn't say any more.

"Anything else?" I asked.

"Yeah. What if there's trouble?" Doody asked.

"We kick ass, what's the big deal?" Kenick said.

"But we're gonna be spread out thin. It could be a problem," Roger said.

"Ahh, you guys. Don't be stupid," Danny said. "This thing is going to be on national television. Nobody, not even the Scorpions, is dumb enough to risk a rumble on television. I mean, shit, that's a complete bust."

"Yeah, don't sweat it," I said.

Everybody had a date lined up. Doody was going with Frenchy, Roger with Marty, and Kenickie had this secret mysterious woman lined up that he wouldn't tell anybody about.

⇜ 26 ⇝

Friday afternoon I took a walk over to the gym, to get a feel for the place before the dance. A camera crew was unloading equipment from a big truck. A crowd of kids watched with excitement. Danny was leaning against the wall, cooled out and taking it all in. I walked over and leaned beside him. In spite of ourselves, we both had a hard time not blowing our cool, 'cause basically we were really up for this.

We decided that we would get dressed together at my house. Danny brought over his clothes and stayed for dinner. Before we took our showers, we went outside and hosed down Finn's Chevy. There was no way that it was ever gonna shine, but at least it was clean.

We were in my room, standing around in our shorts, smoking a last cigarette before we started dressing. Vinnie Fontaine was doing his show. He put in a plug for the Bandstand Dance-off at Rydell.

"Hey, kids, tonight yours truly, the main-brain, Vince Fontaine, will be M.C.-ing the big dance bash out at Rydell High School, in the gym. Along with me will be Mr. T.N.T. himself, Johnny Casino and the Gamblers.

"It's gonna be a live-televised broadcast of the National Bandstand Dance-off, so make it a point to check out the joint. 7:30 tonight! . . . Now, here's one that's climbing the charts like a monkey in a tree. It's already one of the biggest records of 1959, and destined for future gold. . . . 'What I Say?' by Ray Charles. . . ."

Me and Danny were jukin' around my room in our shorts, gettin' loose. It was a mean, hot song and a great one to warm-up to the dance with. Danny and I were singing along with the hey, hey, bop-bop doo-wops, and snapping our fingers.

When it was over, we figured it was time we started getting ready. Man, it felt like our wedding or something. We kept checking each other out each time we put on a piece of clothing, from socks to jackets. My father knocked on the door and poked his head in just as we were fixing each other's tie.

"Hey, you guys would'a made great girls—you're making enough of a fuss."

That was a comment I preferred to ignore but we sure needed his help. "Could ya help us with these cuff links," I asked, forgetting I ignored his help on more ordinary occasions.

The old man was really as excited as we were. He kept straightening things out on both of us—collar, cuff, crease, gig-line, knot—it was amazing how many little details there were to attend to.

"That's what makes it, you know," my father told us. "Details! Everything in this life that's worth anything is a matter of details."

Pop stood back and took us both in with a broad smile.

"Cheez, you guys could sure fool me, if I didn't know any better. I can't remember the last time I seen either of you two greasers dressed up. You almost look sane."

"Yeah, but like you said, Mr. LaTierri, you know better, huh?" Danny joked.

I had to admit, we looked like a million bucks—in small bills. Danny was decked, head to toe, in white, right down to his shoes. My father went over to him and brushed off the back of his jacket, then slipped his hand into Danny's side pocket. I knew he was sliding him some bread, just to cover the evening. The old man was really good like that. He knew Danny's people were really a little strapped for bread, so from time to time he'd slip Danny a little dust, and not make a big deal out of it. Danny was really like another son to him.

And me, damn! I should'a been making a movie instead of going to a dance. I was cased top to bottom in black, looking like a limo. I broke it up with a white silk tie the old man had bought for me, and it was a perfect touch—an important detail, like the old man said.

"You guys look like you just stepped out of a Dick Powell set, no kidding."

Yeah, Pop just couldn't get over us. He came over, put his arm around me and gave me a little hug. I felt his hand sneak into my pocket before he pulled away from me.

Downstairs, my mother was waiting with her Brownie. She took some shots, then got a little misty. She was like that.

"Oh, Sonny," she said, wiping a tear. "What am I going to do at your graduation, or your wedding, if I get like this when you put a suit on to go dancing?"

"Well, Mrs. L.," Danny said to my mother, "to be truthful, I think you better not buy a new dress for graduation, not just yet."

I slugged Danny in the arm. That was just what the old lady needed to hear. We got ourselves together, for the last time, and headed out the door.

"Listen, Sonny," Pop said, "be careful with your cousin's car, and have a great time. And don't worry about getting home, as long as you're in good shape. I'll make sure Mom gets to bed."

Pop was a champ. We pushed off, but before we left, Danny gave my father a hug. I looked at him a little strangely, not for anything except that I was surprised.

Danny smiled and said, "Hell of a guy, ol' Joe."

The top was down, and we were cruising. We stopped to pick up the flowers, and we made a quick hit at Skippy's for a couple of pints of whiskey to dump in the punch.

It was a perfect night—crisp, clear, and cool. We turned on the radio and blasted "Stagger Lee" by Lloyd Price as we wheeled over Oregon Avenue toward Marsha's. Sandy and Marsha had both dressed over there, so we only had one stop to make. We weren't crazy about making the scene with two sets of parents in one night, so we had convinced Sandy to go to Marsha's. We turned onto Marsha's street just as "Back in the U.S.A." by Chuck Berry came on the radio, which forced us to drive around the block until the song was over. You just don't stop driving in the middle of a song like that, it's that simple. Hell! Music, wheels, wind in your hair, whiskey and money in your pocket, and women on the way— was there anything else in life? If there was we didn't know about it, or care.

Marsha's mother opened the door. She was a neat little redheaded lady, who was pretty funny and liked me a lot. She said that I reminded her of herself, when she was my age. I was never really sure what that meant, but it got me over on her, so I didn't really care.

Marsha and Sandy were upstairs when we got there. Me and Danny stood around in the living room in front of a big mirror, primping again. Looking good was beginning to be a pain in the ass. Marsha's mom took more pictures of us, combing our hair, and whatnot—candid shots she called them—then went upstairs to hurry up the girls.

Marsha's mom was the first one down the stairs. She hummed the wedding march and waved her arms. Me and Danny smiled politely, but really wanted to die, it was so dumb. Anyway, those are the things you put up with when you have to deal with parents.

Sandy came down next, then Marsha. God! I hate to say it, but they looked almost as good as we did. We were with the two best-looking girls in the world. Sandy was dressed in this silky white dress with folds and ruffles, and had her hair up with bows in it. She was a living doll. Next to Marsha, they looked like a set. Marsh wore a brilliant daisy-yellow dress, with a low-cut neck and spaghetti straps. The dress was crimped at the waist to accent her hips, then bellowed out over about a hundred slips. Her hair was in a ponytail with little yellow bows. She was a vision of loveliness, and I told her so. It's the truth, I couldn't believe how beautiful she was.

"Marsh, you're gorgeous. Really!" I took her hand. It was the first time I had ever said something like that to a girl and meant it. I wanted to kiss her, but her mom was right there, camera and all.

Danny and Sandy were eating each other up with their eyes. They held hands and were lost. I looked in the mirror and saw all four of us. It was almost enough to make you wanna pack in your leather and go straight.

Marsha's mom got us together for "a few pictures," she said—of the girls, each couple, the guys again, the gang, putting on corsages, putting on carnations, then Marsha, Sandy, Danny and me separately, and finally, the one of us going out the door waving good-bye. Ahh.

It was good to be back in the car and moving. That was a feeling better than anything. Moving in a car, on your way out—really out—with a woman at your side—that was the best.

WE SPENT SOME TIME CRUISING AROUND TOWN, LIS-
tening to music and just enjoying the ride, until we
figured it was time for us to head over to the gym.

When we got to school, the parking lot was already
almost full. It was going to be a good crowd. Some
kids were still hanging around in their cars on the lot,
talking, drinking, smoking, or making out a little bit.
We waited until "Palisades Park" was over, then got
out and headed for the gym.

The place was decorated in Rydell's colors, with a
big banner hanging from the rafters that said, "RY-
DELL HIGH SCHOOL WELCOMES NATIONAL
BANDSTAND." Some kids were in small groups,
others were setting up tables and chairs for refresh-
ments. The TV technicians were adjusting lights and
cameras around the gym. And faculty chaperones
were scattered around the room trying to look relaxed
as they plastered themselves against the walls.

On stage, Johnny Casino and the Gamblers were
setting up and tuning up. Johnny looked knocked out
in his pink and black outfit. Behind him, the Gamblers
were duded up in black and white checked suits. The
band was made up of a guitar, bass, sax, drummer, and
of course, Johnny Casino, on lead guitar and vocals.

Across the room were the sandwich table and punch bowls. At some point soon, I'd have to hit the punch bowls and sneak in the whiskey I'd brought along. Some kids were behind the bleachers smoking. Blanche, McGee's secretary, walked across the gym and yelled into the bleachers, "Names will be taken!" She was scared away by jeers and curses.

"Looks like a pretty good night, huh?" Danny said, tightening his tie.

"*You* look pretty good," Sandy said, smiling.

To look at them, you'd think they were in love.

"I can't believe this!" Marsha said, taking in all the activity around us.

"Ehey, stick with me, kid," I told her. "I'll show you the big time." I shrugged my shoulders, like I had seen Jimmy Cagney doing.

"Yeah," Danny said, "what you have to do is get friendly with the cameraman, Sandy."

"But National TV! This is too much!" Sandy said, gaping. "I hope I don't come off looking silly."

"Don't worry about it, Sandy. They won't be able to take their eyes off me," Danny said, tossing his head back, giving Sandy his profile.

"Nobody likes a camera hog, especially the cameraman."

Danny laughed and put his arm around her. Across the gym, I spotted Doody and Frenchy coming in, with Roger and Marty behind them. I waved, but they didn't see me. We'd catch them later.

A technician crossed in front of us pushing a full-length mirror across the floor. When he passed us we saw that a guy was running along next to him combing his hair in the mirror.

"Oh my God!" Marsha cried.

"What is it?" I panicked and threw my arms around her.

"It's Vince Fontaine!"

"Where?" Sandy shrieked.

"There! In front of the mirror!"

So, *that* was Vince Fontaine—running across the floor like a jerk, following a full-length mirror around. I wasn't surprised. He was tall and skinny, with curly black hair, a grey pin-striped suit and pink polka-dot shirt, with a white scarf around his neck.

"What a jive jerk!" Danny said.

"Yeah, I've seen a better head on a mug of beer," I said.

"Grow up, Sonny," Marsha snapped. "He's neat-o." I guess I touched her in a sore spot. Vinnie was her main stick. Everybody's main-brain.

"I guess he's all right, if you like old men." I couldn't help myself.

Vince caught Marsha looking at him, then backed away from the mirror and laid his Mr. Nice-Guy smile on her, which was really his snake-in-the-grass smile. Marsha melted, then Vince went back to stroking his hair.

There was a guy on the stage who looked official and went up to the mike. He had a hard time turning it on, and jerked it around roughly, then realized that people were watching him. Finally, he got it to work.

"Uhhhh, hi, kids, uhh, teachers, uhh, people. I'm Mr. Rudie, the stage manager for tonight's program. We're going to be on the air in a very short time. If someone in the back would be good enough, please tell those people still in the parking lot and on the steps to get ready. Right now, here are some warm-up numbers from Johnny Casino and the Gamblers."

Johnny came to the mike.

"Hiya, gang. Good to be here for the occasion. Here's a little instrumental number I wrote, called 'Enchanted Guitar'—hope you like it."

The gym was starting to fill up. Kids poured in from the parking lot onto the floor and into the stands. It

was a good time to spike the punch bowls. I grabbed
Marsha's hand, and we left Danny and Sandy dancing
a slow number.

Danny and Sandy were really getting their act together. Lately, Danny had pretty much given up icing-
up in front of Sandy, and to look at them, God!, they
really did look like young teen-age lovers. On the one
hand, it was touching. On the other, it was very funny
to see, in Danny, the future of all greasers going such
a straight and narrow route. It was right out of a
teen magazine.

There were a couple of teachers behind the refresh-
ment tables, but with Marsha there to distract them, it
was no sweat sneaking the whiskey into the punch. She
turned on the charm, smiling, making heart-warming
conversation, covering me with her back, while ol'
Sonny-the-Sneak spiked the punch bowls with two
pints of Old Grandad.

Mr. Rudie came over the P.A. again.

"Fifteen minutes until air time!"

"Can you make it twenty?" somebody yelled up
to him.

Mr. Rudie had a little fit.

"You don't know what we're dealing with here. This
is *live* T.V.," he said, emphasizing the word live as if
it would bite.

If the folks at home were lucky, they just might get
to witness Mr. Rudie having a nervous breakdown on
live television.

Johnny Casino went into a hot rendition of "Rockin' Robin," which brought just about everybody in the
place onto the floor and dancing. Me and Marsha went
out and danced next to Danny and Sandy. We were
all slick and quick and hitting each beat on the head.
Sandy had smoothed out her dancing a lot since the
summer, but, to tell the truth, she was still a little
shaky. Even so, she looked so good to begin with that

it really didn't matter how she danced. All she had to do was get out on the floor and move a little. Just a little. Same was true of Marsha, only she could and did move a lot, and well.

The kids around us were all into the music and picking up the back beat. It was hard to recognize even the kids I knew, 'cause everybody looked so different dressed up. There were a lot of plaid dresses. Red sports jackets were big with a lot of guys. There were also a lot of bare shoulders around the floor, which I had never seen walking the halls of Rydell.

Johnny closed down the rock and roll song and said into the mike, "And for all you slinky dancers—here's 'These Magic Changes.'"

A round of applause went up as Johnny and the Gamblers played the song. Doody and Frenchy were dancing beside us. Doody had his head down and was watching his feet.

"Hey, Doody, can't you at least turn me around or something?" French asked.

"Frenchy! Don't talk. I'm trying to count!" he said, jerking his head up and down to the beat.

It felt really good to hold Marsha close, I mean really close, pressed up against each other, touching thighs, feeling her boobs mushed up against my chest, having my arms around her, and hers around me—it was the absolute best.

Danny and Sandy were folded together next to us, swaying to the music.

When the song was over, me and Marsha got a glass of punch and sat down in the stands. We spotted Rizzo and Jan across the room. They were each holding onto an arm of Leo the Scorpion. I was pointing them out to Marsha when somebody tapped me on the shoulder. I looked up. It was Kenick with his hot, mysterious date. What a friggin' joke! I almost bust out laughing right then and there. Marsha gave me a sharp elbow to the ribs, which helped.

I just couldn't believe what he was with.

"Maybe Kenick should get his eyes examined," Marsha whispered to me.

"Nah, he should get his head examined," I said.

Standing next to Kenick was this incredibly fat and greasy girl in a puffy peachy-pink dress, white anklet socks, and green shoes. From the expression on Kenick's face I knew *this* was his date. Kenick wore a frown that told me, "Ehey, Sonny-boy, times are rough, you know that." I nodded, but still couldn't get over it. I hate to say it but this girl looked like a cartoon. It was too much to be real. And the first words outta her mouth didn't make it any better.

"Jeez, what crummy decorations," she said.

"Where'd ya think you were going—'The Lawrence Welk Show'?" Kenick said to her.

"We had a sock-hop at St. Bernadette's once and the Sisters got real pumpkins and everything."

Marsha leaned over and said to me, "She's a real pumpkin."

"Yeah, that's real neat, Cha-Cha," Kenickie told her. "They probably didn't have a bingo game that night." Kenick turned to me and Marsha. "This is Cha-Cha DeGregorio."

"They call me Cha-Cha because I'm the best dancer at St. Bernadette's, ya know."

"Hiya, Cha-Cha. I'm Sonny. This is Marsha."

"Hey."

"Hey."

Cha-Cha slipped her arm around Kenickie and he jumped about two feet. "Don't handle the goods, ehey?"

"Ahh, ya startin' early tonight, huh Kenick. Wait'll it's time to go, you'll change your mind," Cha-Cha said.

Marsha broke into a smile, and said, "Oh, Nicky, you didn't say that you and Cha-Cha were old friends."

Kenick looked at me and said, with his eyes, that if I didn't shut up Marsha, he was gonna bust *my* head.

Actually, maybe I've given Cha-Cha a raw deal here, because as long as she kept her mouth shut, and had her back turned to you, she wasn't that bad to take.

Kenick was looking around the dance floor when he spotted Rizzo and Jan on Leo's arms. He started to go after him. I jumped up and grabbed him.

"Kenick, don't spill any blood, huh? It makes the dance floor sticky."

"What are you kidding? That jerk shows up with my girl—hell, two girls—and you're gonna let him stand around and look good."

"Kenick, no fights, man. Danny'll have your ass if you start anything. Look man, just cool it and we'll work it out later. You know Rizzo's just trying to make you jealous. So don't give her the satisfaction of flaring up. Hell, you should go over and do something gracious, like say hello, and wish them a good evening."

"Yeah, I'll do something gracious," Kenick groaned, then said, "you're right, Sonny. That'd be just what she'd want, me to bust his brains out—"

"Or get yours busted out," Cha-Cha said.

"Enough," Marsha said. "No trouble, and no jive talk, or I'm leaving."

She was right. Things were cool. Kenick dug it, and smiled.

"You got it, Marsh," he said. "Revenge is best when it's cold, huh?"

Mr. Rudie came to the mike again.

"Five minutes!"

A giant moan went out across the room.

AT THE HOP

Principal McGee came up to the mike.

"Let silence reign supreme!" she said loudly. "First the good news—I'm not grading the dance contest. Now for the bad news—I'm not competing either."

Uggh. I wondered if she really thought she was funny.

Principal McGee continued, "I think we all owe a round of applause to Patty Simcox and her committee for the wonderful decorations."

"Yea! Let's hear it for the toilet paper!" Cha-Cha yelled.

Principal McGee threw her a very dirty look, then said, "Okay, in just a few minutes, the entire nation will be looking at Rydell High School—God help us!—and I want you to be on your best behavior!"

"No hinie biting!" Kenickie yelled.

McGee ignored him. "And now! The moment we've all been waiting for! Here he is! The Prince of the Platters—I can't believe I said that—Mr. Vince Fontaine!"

Johnny Casino and the band broke into Vince's theme song. Vince approached the stage through the middle of a stroll line. He jumped to the stage, and did his rim shot routine.

"Hiya, kids! I'm glad to be at Rydell High."

A roar went up in the gym. It was really a packed house now. Wall to wall kids, bopping and weaving.

Principal McGee took back the mike from Vince, who stood to one side. McGee said, "And now for the rules."

Loud booing echoed through the gym.

"Rule One. All couples must be boy-girl."

"That leaves you out, Eugene!" somebody yelled from the crowd.

"Rule Two. When you are tapped on the shoulder during the contest, you must leave the floor immediately. And the Golden Rule—anyone using tasteless or vulgar movements will be disqualified."

"Well, that lets us out," Kenickie said to Cha-Cha. Everyone on the floor coupled together and proceeded to grind their hips and bodies together, in tasteless and vulgar movements.

"Hey, kids," Vinnie called out, "c'mon. Keep it clean. Keep it clean."

Mr. Rudie took the mike from McGee and announced, "Thirty seconds!" and he looked like he was gonna have a heart attack.

The cameras rolled into position around the floor. Mikes were lowered from the ceiling. Vince took over on the stage, as McGee and Mr. Rudie left.

"Thank you fans and friends and odds and ends . . . and now for all you gals and guys, a word to the wise—You Jims and Sals are my best pals, and to look your best for the big contest, just be yourselves and have a ball, that's where it's at after all. . . ." Vince was really rolling along. "So forget about the camera and think about your beat, and we'll give the folks at home a real big treat . . . Don't worry about where the camera is, just keep on dancing—that's your biz. And if I tap your shoulder, move to the side and let the others finish the ride. . . ."

He was really a sap, but Marsha was digging every word.

From offstage, Mr. Rudie made the countdown. We took to the floor in a stroll formation.

"10. 9. 8. 7. 6. 5. 4. 3. 2. 1. ON THE AIR!!!"

Johnny Casino and the Gamblers ripped open with the National Bandstand Theme. Vince was jiving over the music.

"Hey, hey, hey, and hello . . ."

We were doing the stroll, and looking real good.

Vince continued his rap.

"Welcome to National Bandstand, coming to you

live from Rydell High School. This is the event you've all been waiting for . . . the National Dance-Off. And away we go with Johnny Casino and the Gamblers."

Vince kicked up his leg at the band, and the band broke from the theme song into "Hound Dog" with Johnny doing a mean Elvis.

We broke from the stroll line into a jitterbug. The camera, which had been in the middle of the stroll line panning down the line toward the stage, was swallowed up in the crowd when the music changed. Kids were in front of the camera doing everything they were told not to—looking into the camera, waving, making faces, scratching themselves, and talking to the people at home.

Mr. Rudie was on the floor directing couples to pass before the camera in a steady flow. Wayne and his girlfriend were the first couple, probably 'cause they were both so wholesome looking. But after that, TV-land would have to settle for the rest of us. Kenickie and Cha-Cha, although Mr. Rudie tried to force them off, were the next couple to pass before the camera. Cha-Cha turned her back to the camera, wiggled her fat ass, then faced the camera and giggled.

Frenchy and Doody were next through. Two redheads. A good match.

Me and Marsha followed them, and for the four seconds we were on camera we did pretty good. We were loose as a caboose, mostly from the punch, and shimmied a mean number for the folks at home.

Danny and Sandy followed us. Danny was excited and yelling, "You got it, baby! You got it!" as they juked past the camera.

Sandy looked at him and said, "I do?"

The dance floor was really moving. One camera was coasting along the sidelines of the floor catching all the best of the dancing. On one side some kids were doing the stroll. And scattered around the floor, kids were doing the jitterbug, the duck, and the hully-gully. Me and Marsha started doing the chicken, and in no time we had a whole section going.

The music finally wound down, and Vince came back to the mike.

"All right, and now the event you've all been waiting for, The National Dance-Off! Some lucky guy and gal are going to go bopping home with some terrific prizes, but don't feel bad if I bump yuz out, 'cause it don't matter what ya do with those dancin' shoes. So okay, cats, throw your mittens around your kittens . . . and away we go! Hit it, Johnny!"

Johnny and the Gamblers tore into "Born to Hand Jive." It was a cra-aaazy dance, and one of the ones me and Marsh were the best at. We juked up next to Danny and Sandy and the four of us had a great hand jive going.

Vince was touring through the crowd of dancers on the floor, eliminating couples. Some of the kids weren't really ready to leave the floor, but Mr. Rudie was there to serve as a bouncer.

Danny leaned over to me.

"Hey, Sonny, that chick Kenick is with is a real gorilla!"

"Yeah, that's her over there, pickin' her nose." I pointed across the room, just as Vince showed up next to Cha-Cha and eliminated her and Kenickie.

Johnny picked up the beat, and we started really flippin' out on the hand jive. The four of us got in a circle, clapping each other's hands, tapping hips, heels, flippin' thumbs and shaking our wrists, when Vince came over with Mr. Rudie.

"Ehey, look, you guys and gals are all great, but we got to eliminate you 'cause you're all dancing together, which ain't fair. But Mr. Rudie wants you to keep dancing after we get our winner, 'cause you all look so good, so stay on the sidelines and get ready to come up on Camera #2 when I give you the signal."

We looked at each other in disbelief. So we lost the contest, but we were gonna be showcased on national television. We stood around, tapping our feet and jiving our hands, getting ready to come on. In the next minute, we got the signal from Vince, as he crossed the stage with the winning couple behind him.

We came out onto the floor, and Johnny and the Gamblers started the song from the top again. TV-land was in for a treat, and we gave it to them.

Danny was laying out a hand jive like I had never seen. He looked like his hands were on fire and he was trying to shake them loose. Sandy was picking up the motion, smooth and sexy like. Me and Marsha had a real groovy patty-cake number going, on our knees, hips, and thighs, and were shaking to the left, slipping to the right, and flipping out our thumbs like we were hitchhiking in every direction.

When it was over, we realized that everyone in the gym had circled us. The room filled with applause. We held each other around the waist, and bowed to the cameras and the crowd.

It was a fleeting but great moment of fame. We were pretty knocked out after that number, so we sat in the stands and had the last few cups of punch.

Kenick and Cha-Cha came over.

"Hey," Kenick said, "you guys never told me you could do that stuff. That was a real feature!"

"Naw, nothing to it," Danny said.

"Heck, Kenick, you either got it or you don't," Sandy said, smiling.

We played out the rest of the night, feeling like the real winners of the contest, getting backpats and handshakes everywhere we went. To avoid the autograph hounds, I thought we should leave a little early. Actually, Marsha couldn't stay out that late and I wanted to at least ride through the lakes, even if we couldn't park there, before she had to go home.

After we dropped the girls home, Danny and me drove around the corner and hung out for a while, unwinding before we went home. We lit up a smoke.

"Eh, you know, Sonny, we went crazy for a long time, and this thing was really only another dance."

"What are you kidding me? We were on television!"

"Yeah, I know. I was excited at the time, but we didn't get to see ourselves, and that's the only kick I can think of about being on television."

"Still, it was the best dance Rydell ever had."

"True. I guess what I'm really feeling is a little letdown that it's over, and here it is again down to you and me on this corner, late at night, smoking cigarettes, talking about the night we just had."

"Yeah, I know what you mean, Danny. It always gets down to you and me. I wonder what'll happen to us when we don't have each other anymore."

"When's that?"

"Oh, you know, whenever . . ."

"Yeah, whenever . . . I don't know. But I can't really picture us without each other. It's like breaking a set, right?"

"Right."

"I got the yo-yo . . ." Danny said, and waited for me to fill in the rest of the line we had been running at each other since we were kids . . .

"And I got the string," I said. We slapped each other's hands.

The following Monday, when we were back in school, me, Roger and Kenickie were in Auto Shop working on Greased Lightnin' when Principal McGee came over the P.A. system with an announcement.

"We have pictures of you so-called 'mooners.' And

just because the pictures aren't of your faces, doesn't mean we can't identify you. At this very moment these pictures are on their way to Washington where the FBI has experts on this type of identification. If you turn yourselves in now, you may escape a federal charge!"

We looked at each other and laughed. That lady was really incredible, and always full of surprises. Roger stuck his head out from under the engine and said, rubbing his ass, "I wonder what it looks like blown up on TV."

RUMBLE

when kids usually showed up for the Thunder Road
races. Cars began zipping out of the tunnel and picking their spots along the track. Most of the spectators

193

~ 28 ~

KENICK DID IT. HE CALLED OUT LEO AND THE SCORPI-
ons. He said, "Either you punks clear out of our
neighborhood and leave our women alone, or we take
it to the streets for a fair one."

Leo had been sitting in Hell's Chariot outside the
Palace at the time, when Kenick gave him the word.

"Be here nine tonight, or don't come back at all,"
Kenick said, throwing in, "Ya friggin' pussies."

Kenick could be a scary mother when he wanted to
be. He had his leather hanging off his shoulders and
his fists clenched, and had fire in his eyes. When he
got pissed, he got crazy. A pissed-off crazyman will
do anything in a fight and win every time. He's a
sure bet.

Even though Leo had three Scorpions in his car
with him, one look at Kenickie told him not to get
out of the car. Me and Kenickie were alone in front
of the Palace when Kenick called Leo and the Scorpions out. I guess Leo figured anybody crazy enough to
take on 2 to 1 odds was pretty sure he'd kick your
ass, so Leo just nodded and wheeled out.

"Ya know, Sonny," Kenick said, "that guy could
make a killer outta me, no kidding. He brings out the
worst in me, and makes it feel good. A killer, that's

what I am at times like that. And nobody screws around with a killer—not even another killer. We'll wipe their asses on the sidewalk tonight, just you wait and see. . . ."

So it looked like we were up against our first big rumble. Like I said, we weren't fighters. On the corner we had written on the wall, "Keep your feet as quick as your tongues"—that was how we got by. But Kenick was right, we couldn't let the Scorpions move in on us. It was a question of honor, and territory. If those guys wanted to hang out at the Palace and were decent about it, that would have been cool. But their attitude was more like they wanted to take it away from us, rather than share it, and that *wasn't* cool. Besides, they were snakes. No, worse—worms. In spite of all the shit anyone could say about the Thunderbirds, what they couldn't say was that we weren't nice guys. Sure we could be crazy, and inconsiderate, and loud and rowdy—but basically we were all nice guys. That was why the Pink Ladies dug us—none of us were the world's most ideal guys, by a long shot, but we were all in our own ways lovable guys. So now the lovable guys had to go to war.

Me and Kenick decided we would wait at the Palace for the rest of the T-Birds and clue them in on what was up for tonight.

Doody was the first one to come around.

"What's shakin', Birds?" Doody asked. "You look like you're looking for trouble."

"We already seen it," I said.

"We gotta rumble with the Scorpions. Nine tonight," Kenick said.

"No lie? Tonight? How come?"

"Mostly 'cause they need to have their asses kicked, but they been making moves on us."

"You mean Leo and Rizzo?" Doody asked.

"Well, it's that, but it ain't. Let me tell you, and

Sonny will back me up." Kenick looked at me for assurance. I nodded, even though I didn't know what he was about to say. "Like, at the dance, right? Leo shows up with Rizzo and I'm the better man about it. I let it slide, knowing that if Rizzo got a brain in that beautiful body of hers, she's gonna come back to me soon as she thinks about it. If she don't, then I don't want her anyway, right? So, I'm feeling pretty mature about the whole thing, when the next day I get the word that Leo is pissed 'cause I showed up at the dance with Cha-Cha."

"You mean Godzilla?" Doody asked.

"Yea. Well, it turns out she goes out with Leo, like Rizzo goes out with me. No steady shit, but she's his girl, I guess. But Leo gets pissed, so I decided to call him out."

"Ehh, Kenick, I understand that part, but how did this turn into a rumble? I mean, you and Leo could'a settled this between yourselves, huh?" Doody said.

"Yeah, I suppose, but when I called him out he had his boys with him, so I decided we should do them all in, and get it over with. And Sonny backed me up, so we're on for tonight. Pass the word."

Just then Danny ran up in his track uniform, with a number 4 on his jersey and a relay race baton in his hand.

"Ehey, Zuko, whaddah you doing in your underwear?" Kenick asked him.

"It's my track suit, and I'm in a race," Danny said, panting.

"Well, it's a good thing you're here. We're supposed to rumble the Scorpions tonight," Doody said.

"What time?" Danny looked alarmed.

"Nine o'clock," Kenick answered.

"You're kidding? Nice play. I got field training until nine-thirty."

"You're talking shit, Zuko," Kenick said. "Sneak away."

"Not a chance, Kenick. The coach'd kick my ass, then can it."

"The coach! What about the Scorpions kickin' our asses if you don't show up?" Doody asked.

"Yeah, well what am I supposed to do, anyway? Stomp on somebody's face in my sneakers?"

"Ahh, c'mon, Zuko, whattaya tryin' to prove with this track team crap?" Kenick said.

"Why? What the frig do you care? Look, I gotta cut out now. I'm in the middle of this race." Danny was looking over his shoulder.

"You got the hots for that cheerleader or something?" Doody asked.

"How'd you like a fat lip, Dood? Nine o'clock, huh? I'll be here. Later!" Danny flipped the baton and took off.

"Next thing you know, he'll be gettin' a crew cut," Kenick said.

"C'mon, Kenick, you know Danny's straight up, down to the bone. Give him a break," I said.

"Yeah. Let's go eat something."

"Yeah, what about a knuckle sandwich?" Doody joked.

"Listen, Dood. That might be the main course tonight," Kenick said.

After we ate, we broke up and went home to check in. When I got home, I went downstairs to do some last minute repairs on my zip gun. I couldn't get hold of any bullets, but the gun had a terrifying look to it without the bullets, I thought. Besides, in all the rumbles I had ever seen, there was actually very little beating going on. Mostly, there was a lot of cursing and pushing and nasty talk about each other's mother. I think there was something more to acting out a rumble than actually rumbling.

That's not to say that there weren't a lot of gangs that didn't take their rumbling seriously, 'cause there were. Most of the gangs east and north of us were fighters, knifers, and killers. But our part of town was just too cooled out for that. Nobody cared that much about anything, except their own good looks, which kept our neighborhood pretty quiet. The Scorpions had been known to rumble, but racing cars was more of their thing. As for the Thunderbirds, our rep had it that we were bad, and not to be messed with, so we never had to fight to prove it. No one was that interested in taking us on, not even the Scorpions. But Kenickie was right in going after them. You can't let guys like Leo get away with too much cheap stuff, otherwise they'll start crappin' all over you.

I mean, what we really cared about was girls, music, and each other. We'd kill to protect those things, but fighting wasn't really cool. I think the Pink Ladies had something to do with us not getting caught up with the rumblers. Rizzo said rumbling was for punks, and if we wanted to hang at the Palace with the Ladies, then we had to give up wanting to be punks to be cool.

But I guess there comes a time in even the most peaceful guy's life when he has to put up his hands and fight. Tonight was that time. I packed my zip into my belt under my leather, and left the house looking and feeling like a mean, lean bad ass, dressed completely in black, with shades and a hat.

— 29 —

WHEN I GOT TO THE PALACE, KENICKIE WAS LEANING against the wall in the parking lot, with a big lead pipe in his hand.

"How's it goin', Sonny?" Kenick was also wearing his shades, his leather, a black T-shirt, and black bandanna around his neck. The Thunderbirds were ready to fly. The only problem that I could see was that it was getting very close to nine o'clock and so far it was just me and Kenick to fight whoever showed up from the Scorpions.

"I feel like Custer in the valley, Kenick, waiting for the Indians to come riding down on us," I told him.

"Where's your weapon?" he asked.

I opened my leather to expose my zip gun.

"Hey, that's really good, Sonny. What Cracker-Jack box did you get it out of?"

Shit, I lost all my confidence.

"I made it in shop. Don't it scare you?"

"Yeah, I'm terrified, especially when I look at the yellow string holding it together." Kenick shook his head.

"Well, maybe from a distance. It's only supposed to have dramatic effect anyway."

"Yeah, I can just see the tragedy now . . ."

I leaned against the wall next to Kenick. We touched shoulders, keeping a lookout in different directions.

Doody popped out from behind a parked car in the lot, swinging a baseball bat.

"What time is it? Where are they? Did I miss it? You guys alright?"

It was a bad sign that Doody was worrying about everything at once, when he could see that we were just hanging out trying to psyche ourselves up for this thing.

"Relax, Dood, and take your post. Check the side, we don't want 'em sneakin' up on us." Kenick took off his shades and slipped them in his pocket. "I don't see how you can see anything at night wearing those shades, Sonny."

"That's just the point, Kenick."

Doody was posted at the corner of the lot, while me and Kenick leaned against the back of the Palace checking cars pulling in and out.

"Hey, Sonny," Doody called. "Looks like they ain't gonna show. They said they'd be here at nine, right?"

"What time is it?" I asked.

"Hey, man," Dood called back looking at his watch, "it's almost five after . . . c'mon, let's haul ass."

"Wait a minute," Kenick said, "give 'em another ten minutes. What the hell happened to Roger, anyway?"

"Who cares about lard ass. He wouldn't do us any good anyhow," I said.

"Yeah, but who'da ever thought Zuko would punk out on us," Doody said.

"Nice rumble, huh? A friggin' herd of Scorpions against you, me, and Howdy Doody." Kenick was getting disgusted.

"Hey, you guys, I heard about this one time when the Scorpions were suppose to rumble the Water

Tower Gang and they pulled a sneak attack by drivin'
up in a stolen laundry truck!" I yelled, looking around.

I guess we were all getting a little bit spooked, just
as Roger came charging in completely panicked, waving a car antenna in his hand and shouting, "Okay,
where the frig are they?! I'm gonna bust head and
kick ass!"

"Well, look who's here," Kenick said. "Where ya
been chub-nuts?"

"Hey, Nicky, bite the weenie. My old man made
me help him paint the goddamn basement. I ran out
on him. I couldn't even find my bullwhip so I had to
bust off an aerial."

"Yeah, and whaddah ya expect to do with that
thing?" I asked him.

Doody grabbed Roger's antenna and imitated a
newscaster on the scene.

"Good evening, folks! This is Dennis James bringing you the play-by-play of championship gang fighting, live! Stay tuned 'cause you never know who'll bite
the dust or live to tell about it . . ."

Roger grabbed his antenna back.

"Yeah, well, listen," he said, "I'll take this over any
of those tinker toys you guys got!"

Kenick approached Roger.

"Oh, yeah?" he said. "Okay, Roge, how 'bout if I
hit ya over the head with that thing and then I hit ya
over the head with my pipe and you can tell me which
one hurts you more—okay?" Kenick smiled.

"Okay, ya creep. C'mon and get it! C'mon, Kenick,
big man, big mouth!"

Roger started swinging his antenna over his head,
threatening Kenickie with it. Kenick reached out for
the antenna, and Roge took a swipe at him, and almost cut my head off when Kenick ducked under it.

"Hey watch it with that thing, Pinhead!" I yelled.

"Hey, whatsa matter LaTierri, afraid ya might get hurt a little?"

Roge was really asking for it. I pulled out my zip gun.

"Listen, Chicken-Shit, you're gonna look real funny cruisin' around the neighborhood in a wheelchair with holes in your head."

Roger started to laugh.

"Well, why don'tcha use that thing then?" he said, pointing at my zip gun. "You got enough rubber bands and string there to open a stationery store."

While Roge was bullshitting around, Kenick jumped for his antenna, and knocked it from his hand, leaving Roger defenseless.

"Okay, Roge, what now, huh?"

Roger held up his hand over his head.

"You got me, coppers. I give."

"Smart ass," Kenick said, handing Roger his lead pipe and throwing the antenna into the street. "Here, Roge, this might come in handy."

Kenick pulled out a switchblade from his boot and flicked it open to show us his cutting power. "You see, it's like this, guys. The Kenick can be a killer, so I sent a little message over to the Scorpions early tonight, saying if Leo shows up he better be ready to die or he shouldn't bother to come. I have a feeling that Leo and the Scorpions won't be coming."

Kenick closed his blade and smiled. He lost the crazy look in his eyes, and turned into dumb little, cute little Sicky-Nicky-Kenickie again.

"That was really using your head, Kenick," Doody said. "Best way to avoid a fight is to talk your way out of it."

"But it wasn't *just* talk, and I think those guys knew it. It was like Jerry Lee told 'em when everybody was givin' him shit—'Nobody cuts the Killer!' "

"C'mon, let's go eat and see the Ladies," I said.

GREASE

We started heading around the front of the Palace when Danny came running up, still in his track suit and shoes and swinging a chain.

"A'right, where're the mothers at?" he growled.

"Well," Roger said, "we kicked their asses within an inch of their lives—"

"And, made them apologize to us—" I added.

"And, they promised they'd stay clear of us and the Ladies—" Doody said.

"And, they left here thanking us for sparing them, but said you were a faggot for not showin' up," Kenick concluded.

Danny looked around at each of us, then broke into a smile, seeing that the heat was off and we were okay.

"They know better than to frig around with us, huh?" Danny said. "I mean, what we got the most of is determination—and that's enough to keep things cool down here, ehh?"

"And you know why, don'tcha Danny?" Kenickie asked. " 'Cause *Nobody* cuts the Killer," he said.

DRIVE-IN, WALK OUT

‒ 30 ‒

JUST WHEN YOU THOUGHT THINGS WERE GOING GOOD, that's when you would turn your head for a minute and—look out!—before you knew it you were dropping back to punt. It happened with Marsha and Sandy. They must have been in cahoots because me and Danny got the same message in the same day—we were spending too much time hanging with the guys and not enough time with Marsha and Sandy.

Man, I swear, I really don't know what these chicks wanted, I mean, you give them your heart and they ask for your blood. You can't win. Me and Danny decided that we didn't really have a choice in the matter. We had to take them out, so we decided we would double-date.

The way me and Danny had it figured, we saw Marsha and Sandy just about any time we wanted over at the Palace, and it didn't cost us any bread to take them out, except for maybe a shake or burger we'd spring for in the Palace. Otherwise, we'd hang over there with them, go out in the back and make out in somebody's car, and then split. It was cool, and no distortion. And we saw them when we wanted. Now, all of a sudden, they're getting ideas.

"They're watchin' too many movies," Danny said. He was rubbing his forehead, thinking hard.

"That's what it's got to be—movies. I mean, yooh, Sonny, where else you think all of a sudden they're gonna pick up and start tellin' us what to do? It's got to be the movies!"

"I don't know, Danny," I said, sitting down on the corner steps. "It could be that, then it could be something else."

"Yeah, like what?"

"Books, or their mothers."

"Naw, from what I see with my sister, girls don't talk much to their mothers. It just looks like they do 'cause they do a lot of the same things their mothers do, but they don't really talk about things that count."

"Well, I see a lot of these paperback books where somebody like Connie Francis will sit down and tell these girls just what they should be doing with their guys. It's bad for us, man. Bad. I mean, how the hell do we know what they're being told?"

Danny looked worried.

"We could always buy one of those books . . ." he said.

"Then we'd have to read it. Nix on that." I knew Danny hadn't thought of that. Reading a book was out—o-u-t.

"Yeah, right. We'll handle it some other way. But right now, what about right now?"

"We take them out, what else? Make them happy. Hell, what's the big deal, we'll have a good time like we always do."

"You're right. I just don't like the idea of them calling the shots. Where we gonna go?"

"Where else, the drive-in. I'll get Finn's car, he owes me 'cause I covered for him when he got busted by his girlfriend last week. I said he was with me and our cousin, who was really this other chick he was with."

"Great. I guess we should go to the 61st Street Drive-In, instead of the Airport. They might remember us from the last time we were there, huh?"

"Yeah. I'll call Marsha, and you call Sandy. Tell her we'll pick her up around 7:30."

When I picked up Danny he was smiling the kind of smile I had seen on the faces of the people in a film we saw in health class on crazies. It was a calm and peaceful smile, as if he had lost his mind.

He got in the car beaming.

"Sonny, I'm gonna ask Sandy to go steady. I made up my mind."

"You mean you lost it."

"What are ya sayin'?"

"I'm just joshin' ya, man. I think that's great. Funny. I been wanting to ask Marsha the same thing. I just don't know if she'll go for it. Who knows, huh?"

"That's just what I told myself, Sonny-boy. And besides, I'm a changed man. Really."

It was true. Danny had changed. For instance, he really took that track team stuff seriously. He had more ambition than ability, but he still was taking it seriously. And he had stopped messing around with so many girls. I figured, after thinking for a minute, that Danny should go even further.

"Do it!" I said.

"What?"

"Marry her."

"What?"

"Marry her, Danny."

"Who said anything about getting married? I just said I was gonna ask her to go steady."

"Yeah, so what's the next step, right? Marriage. Why not just ask her now and get it over with?"

I was breaking his chops, just for the hell of it, and he finally caught on.

"Sonny, eat the weenie, willya?"

"Take it out and put it on the dashboard." I called his bluff.

"I would but it's got teeth marks all over it," he came back.

"From what?—are you strokin' it with your old lady's false teeth?"

We busted up laughing.

We were in rare form when we picked up the girls, but they were ready for us. It was one of those nights when everything struck everybody as funny.

"God," Sandy said, "we're all so childish . . . and it's so much fun!"

"Yeah, ain't life wonderful?" Danny sneered.

"A bowl of cherries," I said.

"Ol' sour grapes, LaTierri and Zuko, here," Marsha said.

The 61st Street Drive-In was packed, so we had to park at the back, in front of the concession stand, which had kids hanging out and walking back and forth by it all night, but it was the only place to park, so we were stuck. The movie, *High School Confidential,* was already on when we got settled.

Marsha was being very quiet. Danny and Sandy were in the back holding hands. I put the radio on softly and moved next to Marsha and put my arm around her and whispered in her ear.

"You okay?" I asked. She had a funny, distant look on her face.

She just shook her head, saying that she was okay, but meaning that she really wasn't.

"C'mon, Marsh. Talk to me."

"Sonny," she said, fingering my hand. "Sonny, you still like me, don't you?"

"Ahh, Marsh. Like you? Cheez, more than like. Really. Lots more than like, honest."

"Really?"

"Ehey, you know that, c'mon."

"Well, I guess, but sometimes I'm not really sure. It seems like you spend more time with your friends than with me."

"Marsh, we been through that already, right? First, you're my girl. Second, you're my friend. Third, I got other friends who need me. Fourth, don't ask me to put one thing ahead of the other. Whatever comes first, comes first, right? You know you're the one, right? So, why sweat it. When I'm with my friends, I'm with my friends."

"Sonny, you got a way of not saying much with a lot of words, you know?"

"Well, tell me, Marsha," I said, getting closer to her. "What can I do that I'm not doing . . . besides sleep under your window or wash your father's car?"

"Sonny, you're okay, really. I guess it's me. Sometimes I get these ideas in my head, and I can't think straight. I forget what I got, and think about what I don't, and it's confusing . . ."

"Marsh, you're really nice. And a very pretty girl. And I'm crazy about you. I mean, I got a real thing for you. What can I say?"

She smiled a terrific smile. Ahh, she really was a sweetheart. I leaned toward her and kissed her softly on the lips. It was a long, wet, hot kiss, with gasps for air every minute or so. We wrapped our arms around each other, and when we parted from the kiss I did something which I had wanted to do from the very first minute I saw Marsha. I think I finally had the nerve to do it, because I never stopped to think about it. Never hesitated, not even for a second. I took her face in my hands and looked into her eyes, and then asked her to go steady.

Man, to tell about it now seems dumb, and melodramatic, but, God!, you really had to be there. I swear, I had hot chills running through my body. A cold sweat broke out. Marsha was filling me up and running through my veins.

She gave me the biggest hug I had ever gotten in my life and then never answered me, but just giggled and kept shaking her head, yes, yes, yes, yes . . .

I think I'm basically a little sappy myself, because it was one of the happiest moments in my life. This girl that I loved, loved me! We went into a heavy, juicy make-out and faded away together.

Meanwhile, in the back, I caught bits and pieces of Danny's scene with Sandy, as they did of me and Marsha. From what I picked up and what Danny told me afterwards, here's pretty much what was happening.

Danny slid over next to Sandy, and Sandy slid over next to the door. When Sandy ran out of space in the back, she folded her arms over her chest and looked Danny straight and fiercely in the eye.

"Okay, okay. What's up?" Danny said, knowing he was in for a bust of some kind.

"You know," was all that Sandy said.

She had him, but good. Danny was probably going over a million things in his head that the words *"you know"* could have been referring to.

"C'mon, Sandy, what's buggin' you?"

"You and Patty . . . you went together," she snapped.

"Ahh, so that's it. We didn't *go* together . . . we just *went* together."

"It's the same thing!" Sandy yelled.

"It's not. Not like us . . . I mean it, Sandy. There's nothing like us," Danny sounded like he did mean it. Anyway, I believed him, but that wasn't carrying much weight in the back seat.

Sandy sighed and relaxed a bit, leaning against Danny, but looked away from him, either at the movie or me and Marsha making out in the front seat.

Meanwhile, Danny was struggling to get a spoon

ring he had made in shop off his finger. He was having a terrible time, wringing the ring from his finger. He looked up to see me and Marsha going at it pretty heavy, then got an idea, as Marsha rubbed her fingers through my hair. Danny combed his ring finger through his hair, slicking down his finger, and in one easy try the ring was off and in his hand.

"Sandy," he said softly.

Sandy turned to him, and Danny held out the ring for her to see. Just as he reached for her hand, he took back the ring and wiped it on his shirt, then held it out to her again.

"Oh, Danny . . ." she sighed.

"Wanna go steady?"

Danny slipped the ring on Sandy's shaking hand. She gave him a peck on the cheek. Danny let out a goofy laugh. I swear the guy was touched.

"It's beautiful, Danny. Can I put some tape on it?"

Danny was just about rubbing his hands together at this point, waiting for some good loving, but Sandy slid back next to the door and held the ring up to the light.

"See," she said, turning the ring, "when a girl holds her standards high, a boy respects her."

It really did sound like Sandy had been reading Connie Francis, no joke.

Danny was dumbfounded. Sandy smiled at him, and blew him a kiss, then went back to looking at the ring.

Danny decided to make his big move. It was like a ballet across the back seat. Through a series of yawns, stretches, and twists, Danny slid next to Sandy and had worked his arm on top of the seat behind her. When he was situated, he faked a sneeze and dropped his arm around Sandy's shoulder.

"I hope you're not getting a cold, Danny," she said.

"Oh, no, no. Nothing like that. Nothing contagious. Just drive-in dust."

Danny and Sandy sat quietly for a moment, then Danny began to notice the steady rise and fall of Sandy's breasts, and he started biting his lower lip, trying to control himself. He was fighting desperately with his better judgment and losing fast. His hand rose up in front of Sandy and hung in mid-air for a moment. In spite of Danny, his hands seemed to know better and were quite hesitant about making the big move. Finally, after a deep breath, and a feeling of resolve, Danny let go and clamped his hand firmly over Sandy's left breast.

Sandy almost died.

"Danny!" she yelled, outraged.

Danny was distorted by this time, overcome with heat, and he misunderstood Sandy's scream as one of passion.

"Sandy!" Danny sighed, passionately, taking her in his arms and in one clean sweep he had her lying down beneath him. His eyes were closed in ecstasy as he fell on top of her, and she struggled beneath him.

"Oh, baby, baby!" Danny moaned.

"Danny! Take it easy! What are you trying to do?"

"What'samatter?"

"Well, I mean, I thought we were just gonna, you know, be steadies."

"So, whattaya think goin' steady is, anyway?"

Danny grabbed Sandy again.

"C'mon, baby!"

"Daniel! Stop it! I've never seen you like this!"

"Ahh, relax, willya, nobody's watchin' us. Look-it, do you see Sonny and Marsha having a hard time about it?"

"Danny, please, you're hurting me!"

"Cheez, what are ya gettin' so shook up about? I thought I meant something to you."

"Danny, you do. But I'm still the same girl I was last summer. Just because you give me your ring doesn't mean we're gonna go all the way . . . What kind of a girl do you think I am, anyway?"

"The best, Sandy. The very best. I won't tell a soul, promise."

Sandy threw Danny off of her and climbed over the front seat, opened the door and pulled herself out of the car. Marsha broke away from me and looked at Sandy standing by the car.

"Sandy. C'mon, wait a minute, willya. C'mere," Danny pleaded from the back seat.

"Are you kidding me? I'm not coming back into that, that . . . sin wagon."

Danny couldn't believe it. He looked disgusted.

"Come back here, willya?"

"I'm sorry, Danny . . . maybe we better just forget about the whole thing."

Sandy took off the ring and threw it at Danny, then ran away in tears.

"Hey, Sandy!" Danny yelled out the window. "Where you goin'? You can't just walk out of a drive-in!" Danny tried to get out of the car, thought about it for a second, then slumped back down into the seat.

Marsha was looking from me to Danny and then out the door where Sandy had disappeared.

"So that was it, huh?" she yelled.

"Huh?" I didn't know what she was talking about.

"You guys got together this big plan to ask us both to go steady and then had your own designs in mind for a double-score. Ohh, I get it, LaTierri. You and your sleezy friend Zuko can, can . . . shove it!"

Marsha punched me in the arm and then ran after Sandy, crying.

"Yooh, Marsh. That's not it at all. C'mere, willya?" I called after her and jumped from the car, but she had already run into the darkness and out of sight.

I turned to Danny who was folded in a heap on the back seat.

"Well, Danny-boy, how's it going?"

"Ha. It went. Both ways."

"Yeah."

"Down to me and you again," Danny said.

"Least we got a night out. I mean, we could always be back on the corner. Maybe the movie's not so bad."

"What are ya kiddin' me? Forget it. Let's check out the action. Maybe there's something around here to take our minds off this shit."

"God! I can't believe what just happened to us."

"Yeah. Chicks. Figure 'em." Danny shrugged.

We got out of the car and walked back to the concession stand. Inside, we met up with Kenickie and Doody, who were hanging out talking to a couple of girls from Rydell.

"Ehey, why's everybody look like somebody died tonight?" Doody asked when we walked up.

"Bad news all the way around, back, and home again, Dood. Don't even ask."

"You too, huh?" Kenick said, looking as sad as I had ever seen him.

"Man, you are a bad sight, Nicky," Danny said, putting his arm around Kenick's shoulder. "What's up pal?"

"Rizzo. I just heard she's pregnant. And I didn't even get to hear it from her. Whadda ya think of that?"

"Wow. Bad news comes in bales, don't it?" I said.

The girls from Rydell must have gotten tired of hearing us groaning and crying on each other's shoulders. They flaked off before they even said good-bye.

Just then, Rizzo and Marty came into the concession stand from outside. Kenick caught sight of Rizzo before she had a chance to turn around and walk out. He walked up to her and attempted to look unconcerned.

"Hey, Rizzo. I hear you're knocked up," he said.

Rizzo froze, then turned with hatred in her eyes on Marty. "Boy," she said with contempt, "good news really travels fast." Rizzo turned to face Kenickie. "Yeah, well, you heard right, anyway."

Kenickie couldn't keep his cool anymore. Everybody knew he really cared about Rizzo—everybody except Rizzo.

"Hey, Riz, listen, why didn't you tell me?"

"What's it to ya?" Rizzo had a hard time softening her edges.

"Uhhh, is there anything I can do?" Kenickie asked.

"You did enough."

"C'mon, Riz, you know me well enough to know that no matter what my faults are, I don't run away from my own mistakes. So, let's talk about it, huh?"

"Don't worry about it, Kenickie. It wasn't your mistake, anyway. It was somebody else's."

That dropped on him like a bomb. He was flooding, and was about to say something when he looked around and realized that we were standing around listening to everything as it was coming down. He pulled himself together, barely, and shrugged his shoulders.

"Thanks a lot, kid," he said, then walked out.

Rizzo watched him go, and for a minute I thought she would go after him.

"Hey, Riz," Marty said. "It ain't so bad. You get to stay home from school."

"Just leave me alone, willya? Just leave me alone." Rizzo stormed out into the darkness.

Me, Dood, and Danny walked back to Finn's car and sat for a while just watching the picture and listening to the radio, without talking. It was hard to believe that, inside of half an hour, the bottom had dropped out on all of us. Well, all except Doody, but he was as upset as any of us, just watching what was happening.

Doody was the only one to speak. He said, quietly,

"Cheez, you guys are suppose to set an example for me, you know."

Danny chuckled.

I started the car and eased out of the drive-in.

"Let's go find Kenick," I said. "He's probably walking home."

We drove about a mile and a half, and spotted Kenickie passing under the train trestle at 25th Street. I pulled up and Danny opened the door. Kenick got in, shut the door, and kept staring straight ahead. I don't think he even realized whose car he'd gotten into. We drove home without saying anything.

THUNDER ROAD

~ 31 ~

WE MADE OUR LAST STREET PROMOTION FOR GREASED Lightnin', picking up odds and ends; finishing touches, like fenders. Me and Danny hit on an old Chevy for front fenders and just as we got them off we heard this guy screaming at us. We looked up to see a huge old man running down the street with a bat in his hand.

"Uhh, Sonny, looks like it's time we made our exit, huh?"

"Good idea, Danny-boy. You go uptown, I'll go down, and meet you back at the corner."

We split, and left the old guy standing in the middle of the street looking after us in different directions, wondering which way to go. I looked back before I turned the corner and saw the old man beating the street with his bat.

The next day we finished painting Greased Lightnin', and left her to dry overnight. Word had gotten out to Leo and the Scorpions that the T-Birds were working on their own hot wheels to run off against Hell's Chariot. As a result, word got back to us that the Scorpions would make up for the busted rumble by wiping us out on Thunder Road.

"No chance," Danny said. "But if they do win the

race, then we beat them within an inch of their lives and leave them like toads in the road."

"Right."

"You got it!"

"Friggin' A!"

We all got to Auto Shop early in the morning, but Kenick and Mrs. Murdock had gotten there even before we did. They wouldn't let us into the shop, but told us to go outside and wait by the garage doors.

A few minutes later, the double doors opened and out cruised Greased Lightnin' with Kenick at the wheel and Mrs. Murdock riding shotgun. Me, Doody, Roge, and Danny rushed the car. Greased Lightnin' was a dream.

She was painted a blinding white from nose to tail, with bolts of yellow lightning running along her sides spelling out GREASED LIGHTNIN'. To actually see her in motion was something else. Kenickie looked like a proud father. Mrs. Murdock, the grandmother. And to us, she was one of our own. We could do nothing less than applaud her beauty.

Kenick slowed to a stop, letting the engine purr before shutting her down. Mrs. Murdock got out of the car and backed away from it, giving it the critical eye. She whipped out a rag from her back pocket and gave Greased Lightnin' a few wipes, here and there, then she crooked her thumbs in her belt loops and strolled proudly away.

We stood around congratulating ourselves and Kenickie, as we circled the car.

"This oughta knock 'em outta the stands at Thunder Road," Kenick said confidently.

"You know, you could always change your mind," Doody said. "I mean, she just looks too beautiful to risk in a race."

"Dood, I appreciate your concern, but that's what

all our work was for. In three hours the flag goes down and Greased Lightnin' strikes!" Kenick threw his fist into the air.

"Well, we got it this time, Nicky," Danny said.

"Yeah, you're at the wheel now, buddy," I said to Kenick. "Hit the gas, and kick their ass!"

"You guys should take off. I'll see you at the Road," Kenick said. "I got a couple last minute adjustments . . . Ehhh, Danny, you and Sonny think you can hang around and help me out?"

"No sweat, Nick."

Dood and Roge took off, heading for the Palace.

"Kenick, maybe Doody was right. You know those guys at Thunder Road don't fool around," Danny said.

"Where's your spirit of adventure?" Kenick asked.

"About two steps behind my spirit of survival," Danny said.

"Nicky, look man, we're behind you all the way, either way. So it's on you," I told him.

He thought about it for a minute, looking from Danny and me to his car, then he said, "You guys are something—I mean, you are like the best. Shit, every time I look around for someone, there's one or both of you guys, right beside me. Like that night at the drive-in with Rizzo. That's what good friends are all about, and you guys are good friends . . . so, you know then that I gotta do this."

"Then you're gonna do it!" Danny told him.

"Gonna do it! Gonna do it!" Kenick yelled.

He turned and hit us each in the shoulder, a love tap I guess you'd call it.

"Yeah, well, if we don't win the race, we'll at least win the fight afterward," Danny said.

— 32 —

THUNDER ROAD WAS A STRETCH OF PAVED CEMENT that ran along the river for about a half mile between two bridges. When the docks were being used, it was probably a transport road between them; now it was left for the wharf rats and greasers to tear up. A long brick tunnel from the main street down to Thunder Road was the only access to the race strip.

Along the half mile of track were fragments of collisions and casualties from other races, along with two entire cars, totaled, which were left as judges' booths at either end of the track under the bridges. At the starting line, which was also the finish line, some crates and benches were set up for spectators. But most kids stayed in their cars, or sat on them, to watch the races.

Me, Danny, Roge, and Doody went down with Finn in his car. We got there before anyone. Finn took a few practice runs down the track, testing conditions, he said, then wheeled in and around behind the benches, and pulled up along the side of the track. Finn was a pretty fancy driver himself, but just wasn't that interested in cars.

We got out and hung around the car, waiting for Kenickie to show up. Danny pointed to the tunnel, and we could see a set of headlights coming toward us. The hum of the engine was recognizable, it was Greased Lightnin'. She broke out of the tunnel and wheeled into the daylight like a white metallic bolt of lightning. Kenick spun her around the outside of the track, with Mrs. Murdock still riding shotgun, then whipped her into place right beside Finn's Chevy. We had set up our grease pit on the spot.

Mrs. Murdock got out of the car carrying a case of tools. Kenick opened up the hood and we closed in to make one last inspection.

We heard a rumbling coming through the tunnel and turned to see spots of lights flashing through the dark tunnel behind us. Out of the tunnel roared the Scorpions, packed in three cars with their women, giving an escort to Hell's Chariot, the last car out of the tunnel. It was like a royal procession.

The Scorpions rounded the track a few times, laughing and jeering at Greased Lightnin', but that only made us more determined to win this race. We all felt it. The Scorpions finally wheeled up a few yards away from us, on the other side of the track, and set up their grease pit opposite us.

I got to admit it, Hell's Chariot looked great. It did resemble the devil's machine, which in the case of hot rods gave you a sure winner. The Scorpions started checking out Hell's Chariot, but one look at her told you it really didn't need much looking after. It had Satan's blessings.

Mrs. Murdock was hemming and hawing down in the engine, tapping and screwing here and there, then finally popped her head up smiling. All she said was, "She's gonna win it, believe me." And we did.

It was getting close to three o'clock, which was when kids usually showed up for the Thunder Road races. Cars began zipping out of the tunnel and picking their spots along the track. Most of the spectators were taking the Scorpions' side. We needed some support.

"Where the frig are the cheerleaders now that we really need them?" Danny asked.

The Scorpions had a tough-looking crew just hanging out across the track staring us down. The chicks had close-cropped hair, and were swigging whiskey and mugging smokes, and looking meaner than the guys. They made the Pink Ladies really look like ladies.

Leo and two of his punks crossed the track, with shit-eating grins on their faces.

"So, you guys think you got a winner here, huh?" Leo said, staring down his nose at Greased Lightnin'.

"Know so," Kenick said, squaring around to face him.

"Takes more 'n a coat of paint to make it at Thunder Road. Sure you don't want to change your mind? Punk out?"

"No friggin' way!" Kenick said, not pulling punches.

"Okay. We're racing for pinks," Leo said. His boys smiled behind him. I think they were mute.

"Pinks? What the frig's pinks?" Danny asked, getting testy. He stepped up in front of Kenickie.

"Pinks, you punk! Pink slips! The ownership papers, okay?" Leo snarled.

It was a very stupid move on his part.

Danny gave a soft, but maniacal laugh, which lured Leo into thinking that he and Danny were sharing a laugh together. That was his mistake. Danny lunged for Leo's throat with a monkey wrench, but Kenickie grabbed him from behind.

"The race, Danny. First," Kenick told him.

Leo was visibly shaken. His boys took him back across the track. It was a good move on Danny's part. We needed to shake up those sons-a-bitches and he had them shaking. We also got a cheer from the crowd on the Scorpions' side, grateful for the action.

Just then, Rizzo's pink Stude came out of the tunnel. Kenickie lit up. He watched her pull up. Jan, Marty, and Frenchy got out of the car, then Rizzo drove away. Kenickie's face dropped. He never said anything, but he didn't have to.

Jan, Frenchy, and Marty watched Rizzo leave, then looked at each other in surprise.

"I tell you, Danny-boy," I said quietly, "she's one hard honey."

"Whew, you're tellin' me."

Me and Danny had kind of resolved ourselves to the fact that Sandy and Marsha weren't showing up at the race, and that was that. We hadn't quite admitted that they might not show up ever again, anywhere in our lives, but that was starting to look like a possibility. When Danny put that to me, and asked me what I thought, I told him, "Hell, we'll just have to chase them."

He looked at me with disbelief. "Yeah, we'll chase . . . You kidding me?"

"Danny, you're not being realistic about this whole thing, you know. We've got nothing to lose at this point. It's down to you and me again, so what the hell, man. Take a look around, willya? We got absolutely nothing to lose."

"What can I say to that? You just said it. Put on the ol' track shoes and run them down, right? I knew I was in training for more than a track meet. Like, it's for the rest of my life it looks like."

"What can I say to that? You just said it," I mimicked.

"Yeah, and maybe now that Kenickie's got his wheels rolling, he'll be able to catch up with Rizzo at some point," Danny said. "You know those guys are stuck together, whether they like it or not."

"I think it's wonderful that you talk of love in such lofty terms, Daniel," I told him.

"Sonny-boy, get bent!"

The Ladies came over to our grease pit and tried to look excited.

"Hey, hey, hey!" Frenchy said. "Today's the big day, huh?"

"Tear rubber, Kenick!" Marty yelled.

"That's *burn* rubber, Mart," Roger said.

"Well, whatever . . ."

Doody was working under the dashboard and Kenick was rubbing down the chrome. The rest of us were just hanging around waiting for the start of the race—except for Mrs. Murdock who was checking tires and whatnot.

"Kenickie," Mrs. Murdock said. "If she was in any better shape, she'd fly, and that's no lie!"

"Mrs. Murdock," Kenick said, "she's gonna! You just watch!"

Marty came over and handed Kenickie an old dirty penny she picked up in the dirt.

"Here, Kenick, a little something for luck. I found it heads-up."

Kenick looked at the grimy penny and threw Marty a funny look.

"Ehey, whadah ya want from me?" she said. "It ain't the Indy 500, ya know."

Kenickie smiled and pinched her cheek. Marty was good people. Kenick flipped the penny, but dropped it on its way down. As he bent over to pick it up, Doody came winging out of the car, smashing Kenickie in the head with the door. Kenick hit the ground like a stone and was out cold instantly. Danny and me ran over to him.

"Kenick. Shit! Kenickie! Hey, man!"

"He's out completely, Danny," I said, peeling back one of his eyelids.

Mrs. Murdock was on the spot, and doused him with some water, which slowly brought him around.

"Ahhh, shit!" Kenick groaned. "I'm seeing double."

"You okay, son?" Mrs. Murdock asked.

"I think so, but I don't think I'll be able to drive . . . Where's Danny?" Kenick had panic in his voice.

"Right here, pal. Right here." Danny grabbed Kenick's hand.

"Sonny???" Kenick called, trying to look around.

"Here, pal. Here." I grabbed his other hand.

"We can't let everybody down. You know that. We worked too hard."

"What's the problem?" I said. "Shit, we'll get some ice for your head and by the time the lump goes down, Danny will have won the race. Right, Danny-boy?"

"Friggin' A!" Danny said, straightening up. "Don't worry about a thing, Kenick. Hell, man, if you can't count on ol' Danny Zuko, then forget about arithmetic, 'cause you can't count on nothing then."

Danny helped Kenick to his feet. The Ladies took him over to a bench, and sat with him, wiping him off with cold water. He just looked a little shaken up, but all right.

Danny got into Greased Lightnin'. I rode with him to the starting line. Leo pulled up next to us in Hell's Chariot.

"A'right, the rules are—there ain't no rules. It's to the bridge and back and the first one who makes it here wins. Got it?" Leo growled.

"Ahh, ya punk, you're looking at the winner," Danny said coolly.

"You ain't gonna see me for dust, Zuko," Leo snapped.

Mrs. Murdock walked up to Danny and patted him on the head and said, "Haul ass, kid," then walked over to join the Ladies before Danny could react.

"Ehey, LaTierri, call it!" Leo shouted.

GREASE

I stepped between the two cars as they revved up and quivered beside each other. I looked at Hell's Chariot and saw the devil behind the wheel. Danny sat in Greased Lightnin', steady and ready to blow his barrels.

I raised my arms over my head, looked quickly to each driver, then snapped my arms to my sides. The cars roared away screeching.

Lightnin' and the Chariot fishtailed out at the start, then whipped into a dead heat in the straightaway. Leo veered sharply to the right trying to force Danny into the river. Lightnin' took a bump, but tightly held the road, unfazed by the Chariot.

Dust and dirt was whipping up around the cars. The crowd along the track was yelling and screaming as the cars bumped and cut each other out. It was a dangerous game that Leo chose to play.

When they came into the turn under the bridge, Leo tried to cut Danny out, but Danny braked quickly, letting Leo pass in front of him as he turned, then cut behind him to come out of the turn in the lead.

Leo came out of the turn bearing down for the kill. His boys and chicks were screaming for blood. The Chariot was tailgating Lightnin', tapping Danny's bumper, trying to push him off the road. Danny was forced up onto the rising curve of the dirt roadside, but held Lightnin' under control. He rode the dusty incline for a few seconds, then whomped straight down its side to overtake the Chariot again.

With less than a quarter mile left, the Chariot made its last move to recover the lead. Leo swept in from the left and behind Danny, attempting to force him off the road onto a dock or into the river. Danny bumped bumpers with Leo, moving closer to the dock and the water with each thump. Then, Danny dug down somewhere in Greased Lightnin' and came up with a burst of raw horses. He roared out and away from Leo as Leo swung the Chariot over for what would have been the fatal bump for Lightnin'. Instead, Leo skidded off the road, up onto the dock, and down into the riverbank, landing with his tires stuck up to their skirts in muck.

Danny cruised over the finish line smiling. The T-Birds and Ladies mobbed Danny and Lightnin'. The Scorpions walked to the dock and looked down at Leo, who was looking up at them, and they just stood around like that for a very long time shaking their heads at each other.

We piled into Greased Lightnin' and wheeled around the track, cheering Mrs. Murdock, Kenickie, and Danny. Finn broke out a case of suds he had in his trunk, and we all wheeled over to the Palace and had a celebration in the parking lot, leaving Greased Lightnin' on display out in front of the Palace.

When the Ladies had split with the rest of the T-Birds, me, Kenick, and Danny were left sitting in Greased Lightnin'. We were very drunk, very loud, very sloppy and very depressed.

"Funny, how everybody got off on that today. They all went home tastin' it, feelin' good about it, but now that we did our job and it's over, here we are left drunk and down to it."

Kenick was known to get sappy and sentimental when he was drunk. He was an influence on all of us.

"What's it, huh?" Danny moaned. "I mean, what the hell is it? Why ain't we with our chicks?"

"Why ain't they with us?" I wondered.

"Why the frig ain't we together?" Kenick said sadly.

~ 33 ~

IF WE HAD ONLY KNOWN WHERE THEY WERE MAYBE WE wouldn't have been in for such a big surprise. When Marsha finally did get around to talking to me it all became clear. At the time of the Thunder Road race, she and Sandy got together to figure out all of the things that had come down in their lives . . .

. . . "I'm sick of myself, Marsha. I mean it!" Sandy said.

We were down my basement, playing records and feeling completely disgusted with boys.

"Don't talk like that," I told her. "It makes you sound like a loony, like you might do something drastic."

"I just might! I just might! Marsha, I'm so confused, I don't know who I am anymore. I forget who I was, and why. And I don't know who I want to be. It's so crazy!"

"I know, Sand. I know," I told her. "It's like we got to be one person for our parents, another for the guys out there, and somebody else still for ourselves. And all of those personalities clash."

"It's true, Marsh. And I'm done with it! Just hearing you put it that way makes me realize just what's bothering me. It's giving me the willies. I just can't stand myself anymore. Can you imagine what a drag it is to be weird all the time?—even when you're trying not to be. In fact, especially when you're trying not to be—that's when you're the weirdest. Marsha, this is the last straw!"

"Ehey, take it easy, Sandy. There's nothing weird about you. What? You should feel bad because it's weird to be nice? You should want to kill yourself because it's weird to be in love without wanting to go all the way?"

"Well, I don't think I wanna kill myself. Not yet, anyway. But, God! I don't know whether to change schools, neighborhoods, or lives . . ."

"It's Danny mostly, isn't it?"

"Sure. What else? He's a jerk and I'm head-over for him. What's it with you? Sonny?"

"Well, yes and no. Me and Sonny got a kind of understanding. We fight a lot, mostly for no reason, and we make up a lot, which is fun. I'm stubborn, and he's a mule, so sometimes it's hard. Then, we both have a hard time getting around our friends. I miss him a lot, but I know we'll get back together soon."

"Maybe the best thing is to ask my father to take me out of Rydell . . ." Sandy said.

"C'mon, what'll I do without you? You think nobody cares about you? You can't run away. If you really do feel the way you feel about Danny, then you can't run from it 'cause the feeling'll follow you."

"You're right, Marsh. I've got to face up to the problem, and do something. You know, now that I think about it, I think I've been doing this all wrong. How stupid could I be?"

Sandy slapped herself in the head.

"Marsh, call Frenchy!" Sandy cried.

I was a little confused, but I walked to the phone and dialed.

"Tell her to come right over," Sandy said, pacing the floor, and brightening with each step.

"Tell her that she's gonna be part of a miracle! Tell her she's going to play Teen Angel herself! Tell her to bring her makeup!"

Sandy kept spouting off things to tell Frenchy, which I relayed over the phone. On the other end, Frenchy simply said, "Yeah, yeah, yeah . . . what is she nuts? . . . I'll be right over."

So it was then that Sandy weirded-out on being weird. Even though she was about to do something drastic, as she called it, no one except Marsha and Frenchy knew about it, and no one was talking. But for someone like me, who is basically tuned-in, I felt it in the air. Things were about to happen.

TOGETHER AGAIN

— 34 —

THE SCHOOL CARNIVAL WAS SET FOR THE LAST DAY OF classes, along with another real fun event—report cards. I had the best suggestion of all. I said, "As long as we're gonna be playing carnival, why don't we pretend that my report card is a joke—which it will be."

I saw two things in my future—having a lousy time at the carnival because of my report card, and having to go to summer school if I wanted to graduate. I sat by myself for a while thinking these things over, and I decided that I couldn't let this year go by without at least convincing myself that I learned something, even if my teachers and my parents didn't believe it. I decided that one thing I had acquired was maturity, and because of that I wasn't going to let my report card screw up the day at the carnival for me. And besides that, I decided to go to summer school and graduate. It would be a drag of a summer, but it would be an even worse life if I didn't go.

Talking myself into those things made me feel much better, already ready for the inevitable, and mature enough to cope with it. I figured that wasn't a bad year's work, even though it wouldn't show up on my report card. Hell, I just wasn't in class enough for anyone to find out how much I really knew, that's all.

It had been a little more than a week since the race at Thunder Road, and still Marsha, Sandy, and Rizzo hadn't broken the ice. Me, Danny and Kenick spent a lot of lonely nights together trying to talk each other into going after them. But it struck me that as long as we had each other then we could wait it out, which was probably why Sandy and Marsha and Rizzo also were holding out so long. They not only had each other, but they had other guys chasing them. I was the first one to think of that.

"That could be trouble," Danny agreed.

"Yeah, it already might be," Kenick said.

"Well, what are our choices?" I asked. Suddenly, since realizing that I had flunked most of my classes, I had become the intellectual leader of the gang.

"We can do what we been doin' and wait for them to break down, right?" I said.

"Or, we can start looking for other chicks," Kenick said, but without much conviction.

"Or, we can beat tracks to their doors," Danny said, reluctantly.

"Well, there's one other possibility," I said, perking up. "We can decide to be mature about this whole thing and make our come-back move at the carnival. That way nobody actually has to do any chasing since we'll all be in the same place at the same time. But it'll be up to us to make the first move—that much I'll bet on."

Kenick nodded.

"I think you hit on it, Sonny-boy," Danny said.

"How do we know they ain't got guys, though?" Kenick said.

"Ahh, Nicky, what are ya talkin' about?" Danny said. "Take a look at us . . . what chick in her right mind is gonna go for another guy when she can have one of us? C'mon, ya ain't thinkin' straight."

"Yeah, but . . ." Kenick lowered his head, "Riz told me it was somebody else . . ."

"Ehey, Kenick, she's just upset and confused. She needed a little room to think things over. She's had the time and the room. I'm telling you, make your move at the carnival and you got her back." I tried to sound convincing.

We took a ride to the lakes in Greased Lightnin', listening to some sounds, trying to take our minds off of our chicks. Even the radio seemed to be against us, though. We were coming up with songs like "Lonely Teardrops," by Jackie Wilson, and "The Great Pretender" by the Platters, and "You Cheated, You Lied," by the Heartbeats, and just about every other broken-heart love song we could think of, and some that we didn't know. We changed stations, but they were all out to get us. "True Love for All Eternity" was getting shot to hell, right across the dial. Finally, Kenick shut the radio.

I think we were finding out that it wasn't such a big deal to be a Thunderbird unless you had your girl with you to give you wings. Damn, I think we were all a little tired of hanging out. We wanted to be with our chicks, it was that simple.

We stopped at Skippy's and picked up a couple of sixes-of-suds, and headed for the corner to kill off the beer and what was left of the day. Tomorrow had to be better.

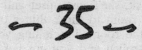

35

THE FIELD BEHIND RYDELL HIGH HAD BEEN TRANS-
formed into a fairground, with rides lining both sides
of the field, and booths zigzagging through the middle.
Banners flew and balloons floated in the air. It was a
carnival all right, and something of a joke.

Me, Doody, Kenick, and Danny walked onto the
field checking out each other's report cards.

"Yooh, Dood, your grades almost spell out your
name," Danny said.

"Well, take a look at Kenickie's, it looks like whoever filled it in was stuttering on "F" all the way
down."

"Shit! I don't believe it!" Kenick said.

"What?"

"How could I have flunked Phys. Ed? I didn't even
know I had it," he said.

There was a booth set up to one side with a sign
that read: "CREAM THE TEACHER—25¢." Coach
Calhoun stood with his head through a hole in a can-
vas drape. Cream pies were lined up along the
counter.

"Hiya, Coach," I said, placing my quarter on the
table.

Mrs. Murdock, who was running the booth, smiled

210

and said, "It's for a good cause, boys—The Teachers' Retirement Fund. Give 'em a pie in the puss!"

The T-Birds crowded around as I picked up the pie.

"C'mon, Coach, let us see ya smile," Danny said.

"Zuko, if you ran your feet as fast as your mouth you might've stayed on the team. As for your buddy LaTierri there, he could use a little mental exercise, too."

Coach smiled and closed his eyes when he saw me cock my arm with the pie in hand. I winged it and it missed him by two feet.

"If you'd have come to class you might've got me, LaTierri!"

"Bite the weenie," I said under my breath, and walked away.

We cruised around looking for the Ladies, and tried to calm each other down. Doody spotted Frenchy.

"Yooh, Beautiful!" he yelled to her.

Frenchy skipped over and gave Dood a big kiss.

"What's hot, lover?" she said.

Doody looked at her and blushed. Frenchy wrapped her arm around Doody and headed off with him.

"French!" Kenick yelled after her, "you see anybody else?" It was his way of asking where the Ladies were.

"Yeah, by the Ferris wheel," Frenchy called back.

Well, it was on me, Danny, and Kenick now. The three desperadoes coming up to high noon. This was the big showdown. We looked at each other, nodded in silence, then headed toward the Ferris wheel.

We walked across the field, around booths and other rides, and it was just a long enough walk to give us a chance to scrape together some last minute confidence, and maybe an opening line or two.

Just as we came into the clearing approaching the Ferris wheel, we heard this sharp and nasty, "HEY!"

We turned and there, leaning against the fence, was

a total stranger. She was a complete knockout, head to toe, dressed in a black sweater, and pink pedal-pushers, and a black satin Pink Ladies' jacket. I took a better look at her face, since, to be honest, it was her swinging body that first caught my eye, and, no shit!, it was Sandy. This beautiful chick, who we had known only as a cute little church mouse, suddenly appeared as the greaser's wet-dream. We stood there flabbergasted, completely at a loss for words. Sandy just stared back, cracking her gum, cooled out, calm, and collected.

She had her hands hitched halfway into her back pockets, pushing out her pointy knockers, and was leaning over to one side, with her hips kicked out on an angle. Whew! I was getting steamed just looked at her. Her hair was frizzed and electric. Her lips were fiery red and ready to be kissed.

If ever there was a greaser's Venus, she was it. I could just see her sitting on the hood of Greased Lightnin' as it coasted up to the Palace.

"Sandy????" Danny finally said.

"Ehey, you got it! How's it hangin' stud?" she said to Danny in a husky voice that sent chills down my spine.

Danny was speechless.

"What'samatter? The great Danny Zuko got nothing to say now that a lady makes a move on *him?*"

I moved aside. This was like a showdown. Sandy looked like the killer. I knew she had it in her all along.

"Uhhh, uhhhh," was all that Danny could manage to say.

Sandy strode over to him and hooked her arm around his waist and pinched his ass.

"Baby, you're the one I want!" Danny said.

"Danny!"

"Sandy!" Danny yelled, throwing his arms around

her. "I got chills . . . I'm tremblin' a lot. I'm nervous and hot . . . SANDY!!! I'm all choked up!"

Sandy laid a long wet kiss on Danny's mouth, then broke into a terrific smile. Danny looked at her and laughed.

"I guess you're still kinda mad at me, huh?" Danny asked.

"Naw," Sandy said, hanging her hands on her hips, imitating a wise-ass, "Frig it!"

Me and Kenick walked off toward the Ferris wheel. Marsha was standing by the entrance waiting to go up. Rizzo was beside her. They pretended not to see us.

"Uhh, you girls want some company?" I asked. I could see Marsha was stifling a smile.

"Hey, Riz," Kenick said softly, "you really shouldn't go on that thing . . . with your condition and all . . ."

"Ahh, ya big palooka, forget it, Nicky. It was a false alarm."

"Wha???" Kenick cried.

"I'm not pregnant!"

"Holy Christ! YAHOOOOO!!!" Kenick ran for Rizzo and swept her off her feet and into the empty basket that was open for the next passengers on the wheel.

"Listen, Riz," he said as they got in, "I'll make an honest woman of you . . ."

"If that's a line, Kenickie, I'm not bitin'."

"It's a bona fide offer, baby," Kenick said, sitting next to Rizzo in the basket.

"Well, it ain't moonlight and roses, but . . . you'll do Kenickie . . . you'll do just fine . . ." Rizzo wrapped her arms around Nicky as the wheel started up.

Everyone else seemed to be teamed up, so it was left to me to bring Marsha around. There was only one way to do it. Be honest.

"Ehey, Marsh . . . I really meant it about wantin' to go steady with you," I said.

Marsha answered before I had a chance to finish.

"Yeah, I realized afterward that it was dumb of me to get pissed at you. I guess you give me so little reason to get mad, LaTierri, that I get pissed at you for what Danny does. I'm sorry. And that's the last time I'm apologizing for it . . . Now, kiss me, you fool!"

Marsha and me were tied up in a pretty heavy clinch when I felt a tapping on my shoulder. I looked up and saw it was Frenchy and Doody.

"Sorry to bother you guys, but we just had to say you look great!" Frenchy said. She was a helpless romantic.

"Yeah, and guess what else? Rizzo and Kenicki are back together," Marsha said.

"And Danny and Sandy made up."

"Gee," Frenchy said sadly, "the whole crowd's together again. I could cry."

"Yeah, me too," Doody said, burying his head into Frenchy's neck.

Danny and Sandy came over, arm in arm, laughing—just as Kenick and Rizzo got off the Ferris wheel. We all stood in a circle staring at each other for a few moments without saying anything. It was a moment of silence filled with love.

"What do we do after graduation?" Frenchy asked, nervously.

"Maybe we'll never see each other again," Marsha said sadly.

"That'll never happen," Danny chimed in.

"How do you know?"

"Whaddah ya mean, how do I know? Tell 'em, Sonny."

"What else?" I said. "We go together."

"The Ladies and T-Birds forever," Kenickie said.

TOGETHER AGAIN

We joined hands and ran through the fairground picking up friends as we ran. Roger and Jan and Marty joined up, and by the time we hit the parking lot Greased Lightnin' was packed with Ladies and T-Birds and friends from nose to trunk. Kenick pulled out slowly and headed for the Palace, while everybody was singing, "Let the Good Times Roll," as we cruised down Passyunk Avenue.

~ 36 ~

So school ended and we had our girls back and we were all in love and everything was terrific. Hunky-dory, right? Sure, we both know better.

Me, Kenickie, and Danny went to summer school together and finally graduated from Rydell without too much ceremony, except for a pretty good drunk we tied on in the parking lot of the Palace with the Ladies.

By the fall, things started changing, too quickly. It was too much to face and keep up with at the same time. We had to look for jobs, clean up our act, and things of that nature which I promised myself I wouldn't talk about here.

That New Year's Eve we had a big party with the T-Birds and the Ladies as we saw the last of the Nifty Fifties—and, to be perfectly honest, I don't think any of us felt all that terrible about seeing that decade and that part of our lives finally coming to a close.